**"I can't concentrate if you look at me that way,"** Paul warned.

"What way?" Caroline asked innocently.

"Don't the men in Beverly Hills tell you how sexy you look when you dance?"

"Oh, yes," she said, teasing him. "Lots of men. All handsome and wealthy."

"So what are they doing while you're in Louisiana?"

She smiled wickedly. "Crying."

"Why? Afraid you'll come back?"

"Oh, you're mean," she said, tapping his cheek playfully.

Paul turned his head and caught her thumb between his teeth and nibbled for a moment before he turned her loose. Caroline's lashes fluttered, and he was irresistibly tempted. He knew she wanted him, and that he could win her over, but he needed time. And the band was starting to play a slow dance. . . .

## WHAT ARE *LOVESWEPT* ROMANCES?

They are stories of true romance and touching emotion. We believe those two very important ingredients are constants in our highly sensual and very believable stories in the *LOVESWEPT* line. Our goal is to give you, the reader, stories of consistently high quality that may sometimes make you laugh, sometimes make you cry, but are always fresh and creative and contain many delightful surprises within their pages.

Most romance fans read an enormous number of books. Those they truly love, they keep. Others may be traded with friends and soon forgotten. We hope that each *LOVESWEPT* romance will be a treasure—a "keeper." We will always try to publish

*LOVE STORIES YOU'LL NEVER FORGET*
*BY AUTHORS YOU'LL ALWAYS REMEMBER*

The Editors

## LOVESWEPT® • 354

# Deborah Smith
# Hot Touch

BANTAM BOOKS
NEW YORK • TORONTO • LONDON • SYDNEY • AUCKLAND

HOT TOUCH
A Bantam Book / October 1989

If you would be interested in receiving protective vinyl
covers for your Loveswept books, please write to this address
for information:

Loveswept
Bantam Books
P.O. Box 985
Hicksville, NY 11802

ISBN 0-553-22014-4

Published simultaneously in the United States and Canada

PRINTED IN THE UNITED STATES OF AMERICA

O      0 9 8 7 6 5 4 3 2 1

*To Pearl, Ruby, Oscar, Emmy, and White Kitty—*
*who talk to me quite often.*

# One

Paul Belue slammed both large, sinewy fists onto the tabletop with a force that sent a shiver through the crowded trailer. He was happy to note that everyone from the producer to the script girl jumped.

"Nobody works with Wolf but me! He doesn't need another trainer, *no*! He doesn't need stress reduction or better vibes! Look, I've had enough! I let you film in my house, and you've turned the whole bottom floor into an obstacle course! I nearly kill myself going to the kitchen! Enough! You're not bringing some silly woman in here to use some sort of silly California techniques on my timber wolf!"

"Dr. Belue, you're yelling again. We agreed that you wouldn't yell," the director said firmly.

Paul glared at a spike-haired young woman, then at Frank Windham. "Cajuns yell!" he bellowed, waving his hands. The crowd of people leaned back, their faces chalk white.

Their silent reaction was what he'd come to expect. Movie people, *poo-yie*! They didn't know how to have a good, loud, soul-satisfying fight. That's why Frank, the producer, suffered from tension headaches. Even now

Frank was rubbing his fingers against the silver-streaked brown hair at his temples.

"We have a contract, you prickly s.o.b.," Frank reminded him smoothly. "And I'm losing thousands of dollars every day that your mutt refuses to work. You have no choice. If you don't let me bring a professional trainer here, I'll sue you up one side of the bayou and down the other."

Paul leaned back in his chair, crossed his arms over his chest, and eyed the producer lethally. "I see."

"A lot of producers swear by this trainer. She's worked with the biggest names in the business—Spuds MacKenzie, Benji, Morris the Cat. Her effect on animals is almost eerie."

"*Bien*," Paul retorted dryly. "A Beverly Hills witch."

"You'll like her. I promise."

Frank was proud of his skill in diplomacy, but he knew he'd just told a whopper of a lie. Inside her small circle of friends Caroline was respected and adored. Outside that circle she was merely respected. He'd seen her reduce troublemakers to shreds, and she was already in a foul mood over this job.

Paul Belue commanded respect in general and something more where women were concerned—slavelike devotion. Every female on the set thought he was part Clark Gable, part Cajun Gypsy, and all stud.

But Caroline wasn't a typical woman. When she got through with him, he'd carry his hide away in little pieces.

"Wolf won't obey anyone but me," Paul informed him.

"Then why won't he pay attention to your commands anymore? You're a veterinarian. Why don't you give him an antidepressant or something?"

Paul rose to his feet slowly, his exuberant anger turning quieter, more deadly. "I'd rather stuff *you* with antidepressants. Wolf doesn't need them. Just give me time to figure him out. He's not as simple as a dog."

"He's half Labrador retriever. Figure that half out while the trainer takes care of the rest."

"Or you'll sue me for breach of contract?"

"Does an alligator have fins?" the producer retorted sarcastically.

"No. It doesn't."

"Whatever. I want Wolf back to peak performance as soon as possible. Come on, Paul, he's going to be a *star*. He's going to make a bundle of money for you. Don't throw it all away because of pride."

Defeat and frustration coiled inside Paul's chest. He needed Frank's money too badly to argue. Damn, the money problem was like a sharp knife always jabbing at him. His temper was frayed because of it.

"All right, *mon ami*," he said in a low voice, his jaw clenched. "Bring on the lady trainer, but *you* be responsible when Wolf chews one of her hands off. And if she causes any trouble, Wolf will be the least of her worries."

Hell would have been cooler.

Caroline Fitzsimmons stared out the limousine's window at steam rising off the ghostly, moss-draped forest from a recent rain. How could a state be so ethereally beautiful and so hot at the same time? She tapped the intercom button imperiously.

"Driver?"

"Yes'm, what can I do for you?" The chauffeur had a thick drawl that grated on her nerves. It was actually a pretty accent with all those lazy vowels and dropped g's, but it stirred up odd sensations that disturbed her because she couldn't quite recall the memories behind them.

"Is everything here covered in some sort of growing vegetation?" she demanded. "If I stand outside too long, will I sprout leaves?"

"Ma'am?"

He had missed the joke. "Spanish moss, vines, etcetera. Is it all like this?"

"Oh. Yes'm. The Cajun country's semitropical. That's why it's a great place for growing sugarcane and rice."

"Lovely," she muttered under her breath. "Sweets and starch." To the driver she said, "What's the temperature this morning?"

"Only seventy degrees. Perfect fall weather."

"What's the humidity?"

"About eighty percent."

"Perfect fall weather if you like to live in a sauna," she muttered. "Thank you."

Caroline flicked the intercom off, slipped a Walkman headset over her ears, and listened to a tape of soothing ocean sounds. Here she was, three hours from the civilization of New Orleans, speeding through a moody, junglelike land of swamps and marshes, while her permanent went limp even in the air-conditioned limousine.

*If the wolf didn't respond quickly, she'd bite him.*

Big Daddy regularly wandered out of the swamp that adjoined Grande Rivage to nap in the plantation's long gravel driveway. Paul suspected that he enjoyed the warm gravel and the shady canopy of oak trees. Or maybe he just liked to hear colorful Cajun curses.

"Lousy 'gator, I should have you stuffed and mounted out here," Paul threatened.

"Where does a twenty-foot alligator sleep?" Ed Thompson asked as they circled the big reptile carefully. "Anywhere he wants to."

"Let's grab his tail. On the count. *Un, deux, trois.*"

They latched onto Big Daddy's tail and spent the next two minutes hopelessly trying to budge the alligator. Paul glanced up at the wiry young black man pulling beside him. Sweat streamed down Ed's bare chest and soaked the waist of his khaki shorts. His face was contorted with effort. "Ed, this is like a pair of flies trying to drag the Loch Ness monster. Let's go get the tractor."

Ed nodded. "They never told us about this in college. Zoology was supposed to be glamorous."

"Nothing glamorous about 'gator rasslin', *mon ami.*"

Paul heard the sound of a car in the distance. He looked down the driveway, and after a stunned moment cursed loudly.

It must be the animal trainer. In a limo. A limo. Even the brat-pack types in the movie had come down from New Orleans in a chartered bus.

"Definitely impressive," Ed commented.

"Ridiculous."

An idea occurred to Paul, and he perused Big Daddy thoughtfully. "Leave him, Ed. Go feed the panthers. I'll take care of this."

"Fine." They dropped Big Daddy's massive tail and danced away as the alligator flipped it from side to side. "Are you just going to let him stay here like an ugly speed bump?"

"I'll think of something."

Ed nodded again, then headed for the trail to the wild animal compound.

Caroline looked up from reading *Vogue* as the limousine came to a stop. She peered out the window and gasped in awe at the magnificent trees that lined the drive. Their massive, gnarled trunks proclaimed great age. She could almost picture Rhett and Scarlett driving past them in a horse-drawn carriage.

She drew her earphones off and punched the intercom button. "Is this the Grande Rivage plantation?"

"Yes'm. The driveway, anyhow."

"It's magnificent. But why are we stopping?"

"There's a man and an alligator in the middle of the road."

Caroline lifted her brows drolly. "They've been run over?"

"No, ma'am. At least—I'm not sure about the alligator, but the man's okay. He waved for me to stop."

"Well, please tell him to move his walking handbag out of the way. I'm in a hurry."

"Yes'm."

She returned to reading. A minute later the driver came to her door and opened it. Caroline sniffed delicately as warm, muggy, sweetly scented air flowed into the car.

"Ma'am, the fellow says, 'De 'gator, he's not moving, moan amee.' You'll have to walk the rest of the way."

"How far is it?"

"Ohhh, couple hundred yards. Picture two football fields end to end."

Caroline lowered her chin and gazed at him solemnly. "I'll consider walking when it's two *tennis courts*." She paused, grimacing. "Is the man Cajun?"

"Yes'm."

She hoped fervently that this plantation wasn't staffed entirely with Cajuns. If her mother's family was any indication, their down-home nobility was one of the biggest media-created myths of the last decade.

Caroline nodded to the chauffeur. "Tell Frenchy that de 'gator, he *is* moving."

"Uh, yes'm, I'll see what I can do."

He shut the door. Caroline shifted anxiously against the limo's seat. She just wanted to get to the plantation house—Frank had described it so lovingly—unpack her things, and stretch out in a cool room.

"Sir, the lady says you'll have to move the alligator."

Paul stared down at the sweating, uncertain chauffeur. "The lady refuses to get out and walk, yes?"

"Uh, yes. She's not dressed for walking, see. And she doesn't like the heat."

Paul inhaled slowly, his fists clenching and unclenching. "Let me make certain before I do anything. This is Caroline Fitzsimmons, yes?"

"Uh, yes."

Narrowing his eyes, Paul looked at the limo and smiled. No Beverly Hills prima donna was going to meddle with his wolf. "I'll talk to the lady."

Caroline fidgeted, wondering what kind of crude, backward man blocked their way. To distract herself she fished through her Louis Vuitton travel bag and selected a pair of wraparound sunglasses with sleek silver frames. She put the glasses on and retrieved a gold compact from the bag.

She was checking her lipstick when her door was jerked open so hard that the limo rocked. Startled, Caroline dropped her compact and twisted quickly toward the invader.

"Haul your butt out of this car, *chère!*"

He had an incredibly deep voice. It was the voice of doom, if doom had a Cajun accent. Her mouth gaping, Caroline stared up at him.

He blocked the sun. He was big, or maybe he just seemed that way because he was so close. He wore only faded jeans and muddy, laced-up work boots, one of which he placed jauntily on the edge of her door like a challenge.

Caroline blinked rapidly and swallowed. Her mind took control of her gaping mouth and snapped it shut. She reached behind her on the seat, clasped a white umbrella with black polka dots, and brandished it at him like a club.

"I don't know what swamp you crawled out of, but go back to it," she ordered. "I'm here on business. You've obviously mistaken me for someone who enjoys the odor of sweat and dirt."

Muscles flexed in his brawny arms as he leaned forward. He flashed her a startlingly white smile. It had all the warmth of a dog's snarl.

Thank goodness he was backlit by the sun so that she could hardly see his features. He was overwhelming enough as it was.

"Caro-line Fitz-sim-mons," he said with slow emphasis. "I *know* who you are. And you've come to the wrong place if you think you're going to pull a princess routine. Get out of that car and walk."

Caroline tried to peer past him. Her chest rose and fell swiftly. "Driver! We're leaving now!"

The hulk threw a gaze over his shoulder at her slack-jawed chauffeur. "Don't move an inch, friend."

Mad and more frightened than ever, Caroline jabbed the tip of her umbrella into the invader's stomach. She might as well have poked a brick wall. An angry brick wall.

He glared down at her in amazement. "You just lost all your Brownie points, and you didn't have many."

"Get your boot off my door," she ordered in a grim voice. "Or I'll poke something soft."

The subtle, preparatory tightening of his body should have been a warning, but she missed the clue. She aimed the umbrella at the bulge in the front of his snug jeans.

"Lady, you'll spend a long time looking for anything soft on *me*," he retorted. Then he snatched the umbrella from her grasp, threw it onto the grassy roadside behind him, and reached into the car with both hands.

Caroline's palm connected on his cheek with a loud crack just before he got her by the wrists.

"Out of there!" he yelled.

She wasn't certain how he did it, but he jerked her from the limo with so much powerful grace that it didn't hurt.

Caroline tottered beside the car, the heels of her black pumps sinking into the gravel. He let her go and she nearly fell backward into the seat. Grasping the door frame on both sides of her, she gave in to blind fury.

"Who do you think you are, you backwoods cretin?"

She swung at him with one fist and caught his jaw squarely. Caroline heard his teeth click together with the force of her blow. Her cocktail ring left a tiny cut on his cheek.

Astonishment made his mouth drop open. He raised one hand to his jaw as if to confirm that she'd just hit him.

"I've been kicked, stomped, bitten, and spit on by everything in the animal kingdom," he told her in a deadly tone. "Except a Barbie doll." He planted his hands on the hood of the car, effectively trapping her between his arms.

Caroline kept her fist raised but stared at him in a daze of horror. This anonymous bully was now going to kill her, she was certain. He looked totally uncivilized. His hair was Indian black with only a hint of softer shadings. It hadn't seen a comb recently. Although layered, it was long enough in back to brush the tops of his broad shoulders.

He had a chest full of tightly woven muscles covered in a thick black pelt. At the moment she could imagine him pounding that chest like an angry gorilla.

She drew her fist back. "Step away, you bastard," she warned. "I don't know what you're after, but you'll be sorry you wanted it."

Though he didn't budge, his eyes narrowed lethally. Caroline winced. Why couldn't she have said step away, *please*, you bastard?

"You're going back to California on the next plane!" he shouted. Then he shook both fists in the air and began calling her names in French. They were undoubtedly as unpleasant as they sounded.

He was so dramatic and so thoroughly mesmerizing that she watched him in silent awe. His face was strong-featured and handsome, but hardly pretty. His nose was rather large. But his eyes—his eyes were amazing, such a light blue that they stood out like translucent sapphires against his deeply tanned skin.

"Who are you? I don't care what you think! Shut up!" she interjected. That only provoked him more.

In the midst of yelling Paul realized that he couldn't drag his gaze away from her. She looked upset, but not frightened . . . maybe that was the attraction. Maybe it was her damned calculated aura of mystery. He could see very little of her face.

She wore dark sunglasses and a black scarf with fine white dots. The scarf was wound under her chin and around her neck in a style reminiscent of the fifties. A smooth, straight strand of strawberry-blond hair peeked out decoratively on one side of her forehead.

When he stopped yelling she simply stared at him for a moment. Her driver still stood in the distance, his mouth hanging open.

"Finished?" she finally inquired.

Her skin was flushed with anger underneath a golden tan. Her nostrils flared rhythmically at the end of a short, aquiline nose. Despite the deadly way she had her lips clamped together, they looked luscious.

She smirked at him. "Whoever you are, I'm going to kick your sweating hulk off this place so fast that you'll feel like gumbo in a hurricane."

"You will, eh, *chère*?" Paul raked her up and down. "You're not dressed for anything so physical."

She was the epitome of fashion in a white dress with enormous padded shoulders and a skirt that barely came to mid-thigh. Skin-tight pants extended from under the skirt and stopped just below her knees, outlining extremely pretty legs. The legs, cased in white hose, continued in the same curvaceous way all the way down to her high-heeled black shoes.

"Okay, Tarzan, seen many women lately?" she inquired in a tone that could have frozen a volcano.

"Not any dressed for the circus."

He gazed disdainfully at her knee pants. They had a tiny polka-dot print that matched her scarf. A wide black belt made her waist look too small for her height—she was only a few inches shorter than he was. Paul smiled at the indignant way her lips pursed.

Her chin came up. "A fashion critique from a wild boar is hardly worth considering."

"You look like a piece of candy wrapped up in too much paper. By the time a man got you unwrapped, he'd forget that he was hungry."

"I'm here on business with the producer of a movie. You couldn't possibly work for him. He has good taste. So you must be some sort of hired help at the plantation. Consider yourself out of a job. Now get your lizard out of the road and your face out of my sight."

"Ol' 'gator, he doesn't move for man nor circus woman." Paul turned toward the chauffeur and gestured grandly. "Get her luggage out. Let her carry it. She looks capable, like she takes aerobics classes and lifts weights. With her tongue."

"Pal," she interjected, "you can take your attitude and put it where the sun—"

"The sun shines everywhere down here," he finished dryly. "And it gets *beaucoup* hot for a woman who runs her mouth when she should be carrying her luggage to the big house."

Caroline crossed her arms over her chest. Perspiration was already beading on her scalp. The scarf itched. "Move the alligator," she ordered.

Paul stepped back and waved her toward the front of the limo. "You move him."

The tension inside Caroline's chest lightened as she considered that offer. She smiled at him in a condescending way. "All right."

They walked to where the monstrous, muddy thing lay dozing in the center of the driveway. Her tormentor threw out a protective arm to halt her. Surprised, Caroline bumped into the muscled barrier at breast height.

Tarzan might be sweaty, dirty, and bad-tempered, but he was also a walking catalogue of perfect male parts. The pressure of his arm against Caroline's bosom drew primitive requests straight from her hormones. *We'll take one of those, and two of those, and lots of that . . .*

"How gallant," she muttered, and stepped back. She feigned interest in the alligator. "Well, well, an Izod emblem with teeth."

"Big Daddy likes to chase women. You're not wearing any alligator skin, are you?"

"Oh, just my underwear."

"Seems appropriate."

Her face burned with more than the external heat. Watch this, Mr. Macho.

"Beat it, alligator, before mother nature notices that you flunked the quiz on evolution," she said aloud for effect.

Caroline peered at the reptile with a twinge of performance anxiety. She'd never dealt with a mind quite so primitive. Even frogs were sharper than this.

Big Daddy's large, dark eyes opened slowly. He rose to all fours. He waddled off the road, his body swinging from side to side. She exhaled in relief. Caroline smiled sweetly at the shocked man beside her.

"I'm a professional animal trainer," she explained. "It's all in knowing how to pitch your voice."

Disgust flooded his expression. "Dumb luck."

"No, that's how you get a girl."

His eyes flared with amusement and he whistled softly under his breath. "Hinting for some fun? Can't take you up on it. Might get frostbite."

Caroline grimaced. This was hopeless. "I'm not going

to ask you to tell me your name. Primitive organisms don't have names. But I assure you that you'll hear about this from the owner."

"Already heard." It was obvious that he'd been waiting for this moment. He bowed and smiled with grand satisfaction. "That's me. The owner."

Her back stiffened slowly. Then one corner of her mouth drew up in sardonic amusement.

Watching, Paul gave her credit for having a sense of humor.

"Dr. Belue, I presume," she said flatly.

"*Blue* to my friends." He paused. "But you can call me Dr. Belue."

"Oh, I intend to."

Even behind the dark sunglasses he could tell that her eyes were wide with astonishment over his identity. What color were those eyes? He had an overwhelming need to find out. With a quick, catlike flick of his hand he slipped the glasses off her face.

He'd never forget her reaction as long as he lived. Her eyes—he didn't even notice their color—narrowed in distress. One hand flew toward the left side of her face, then wavered as if she were ashamed of her reaction, and dropped back to her side.

She glared up at him, knowing that he couldn't help staring at the jagged white scar that ran from the corner of her left eye back into the hair at her temple, hating the fact that the good, honest challenge in his gaze softened with pity.

Caroline jerked her sunglasses out of his hand and nearly stabbed herself in the eyes putting them on again. Then she turned the air blue with invective. She'd do anything to make him fight again. Anything was better than sympathy.

He cocked his head to one side and gave her a rebuking look that was even more upsetting because she sensed that he understood her defensiveness.

Shaking, Caroline withdrew behind her icy facade. Her voice dropped to a low level that was at least formal, if not calm. "You're about as likable as a bad fungus, and I'd rather spend time in hell than in this sweltering little backwoods Eden. But I'll survive. I want a room. Your best room, with air-conditioning. It better have a telephone. And I'll give your cook a grocery list. I'm a vegetarian."

Anger clouded his gaze again. "You're a pain in the ass, Mademoiselle Fitzsimmons," he corrected her.

"Precisely. I've had years of practice and the best teachers."

She turned on one heel and went back to the car. She slammed the door and sat in the dim, quiet interior, staring straight ahead, tears glittering in her eyes.

Her triumphant return to Louisiana didn't feel that way at all.

# Two

Her visions of Scarlett and Rhett faded as soon as she saw the main house. This was Tara *after* the war.

"This is a punishment," she said numbly. "I've been cursed."

The driver set her luggage on the patio and waited expectantly. Caroline dabbed at her dewy face with a pink tissue and tried to forget what Dr. Belue had just done to her emotions.

Grande Rivage hadn't been grand for at least fifty years. She leaned against the limousine, staring up at large columns devoid of paint and an upstairs gallery that sagged slightly on one side. Dingy, torn curtains fluttered in the windows. Peeling white shutters hung askew from the dormer windows on top.

But the ghost of majesty was still evident, and she couldn't deny that it appealed to her. A parade of tall doors fronted the house on both stories, and most of them were open to let the breeze through.

The house was sturdily built of handmade red brick; the years couldn't ruin such craftsmanship. A beautiful filigreed iron balustrade decorated the gallery, and huge azaleas nestled against the red-tiled patio that skirted the bottom story. The first floor opened directly onto that ground-level patio.

Thick honeysuckle and jasmine climbed the trunks of overhanging oaks that must have been planted when the house was built. The paddlelike leaves of giant magnolias fluttered in the sultry air. Caroline searched for descriptions that would do the old home justice. Provocative. Romantic.

Then she tried to shrug off such whimsy. At least the lawn was cut—well, in the spots that still had grass.

"Caroline!"

She turned toward Frank's relieved voice. He came across the lawn from a camper's nightmare of trailers, vans, and utility vehicles clustered among a grove of trees in the distance. Beyond the grove she saw white outbuildings, fences, and pastureland dotted with tiny, striped ponies. *What?*

Near the trailers a few members of the crew had set up a volleyball net and were sweating through a vigorous game. Frank trotted up to her, clapping happily, his sandy brown hair ruffled by a warm breeze. But he looked tense, like the movie producer he was, conscious of the minutes ticking his money away.

"Caroline, how was your trip?"

She smiled and returned Frank's hug. Then she held him at arm's length and didn't mince words. "I just met Dr. Belue. He hates me. And I hate him." She quickly told him about the encounter.

Frank's happy expression fell ten feet. Then he shrugged. "I'm surprised it took so long."

"Why does he want to get rid of me?"

"He thinks you're a waste of time. He thinks his wolf will eat you alive. You'll have to tread lightly."

"I'm not worried about the wolf. I'll get wolfie back to work for you, Frank." She patted his back. "Just relax and stop having those migraines. Gretchen's concerned about you."

"I know. I'm overreacting. It has something to do with ten million dollars of investors' money."

"The wolf won't be a problem," she emphasized. "But I can't stay in the same house with the mad doctor. Are you sure there isn't a trailer available?"

"Sweetness, I had enough trouble getting the ones we have. We're not exactly in the middle of civilization, you know."

"An understatement. The road signs to this place ought to read *Nowhere* and *Oblivion*."

"Very funny."

She gestured toward the house. "You said it was charming. So are the ruins of Greece, but I wouldn't want to live in them."

"The torn curtains and peeling paint are our doing. The house was presentable before we dressed it for the film."

"Haunted-house theme?"

"My dear, you obviously haven't read the script I sent. *The Legend of Silver Wolf* is a kiddie flick about a wolf who rescues two children lost in the swamp. He leads them to this spooky old house where a hermit lives. The hermit is really a sweet, lonely old man. Silver Wolf saves everybody from some villains."

She arched one brow. "I met one of the villains a few minutes ago. Terrific casting."

Frank laughed wearily. "I like Blue," he told her. "And I respect him. He's operating this place on a shoestring. He runs an endangered-species habitat, and except for a few government grants, he's pretty much self-supporting."

"Oh? He protects the declining population of male macho mutants?"

"Panthers, Caroline. He's trying to save a rare species of panther. He also works with ferrets and birds, not to mention half a dozen other things. He's a very private man and he doesn't like having us around. But he needs the money."

The sound of running hooves made them both turn quickly. The chauffeur hid behind a column. A half-dozen llamas trotted around the corner of the house and passed in front of them. A young man in khaki shorts trotted with them, waving a short stick.

He waved at Frank. Frank waved back. "Hi, Ed."

Caroline brushed her hand in front of her face as dust rose in a cloud. "Who was that?"

"Ed Thompson. Zoologist. Works for Blue."

"Llamas aren't endangered."

"Blue sells them as exotic pets. There's good money in llamas. He also sells miniature zebras."

Caroline looked toward the pasture. The striped ponies, of course. "This place has everything," she added grimly, "Including one giant Cajun turkey."

"Gobble-gobble," a deep voice said behind her.

She turned slowly, gazed up into cool blue eyes, and smiled. The man was as provocative as his home. "Well, if it isn't Dr. Dolittle."

If she sniffed one more time, he'd throw her out of his house on her designer-clad fanny.

She did it so delicately, barely making a sound. In fact, maybe the sniffing was his imagination. It was just the way she glided around beside him through the large, austere rooms, still wearing her sunglasses and scarf as if she were afraid of contamination. She kept her hands clasped behind her back.

She was conducting an inspection, and she made it obvious that his house wasn't going to pass.

"Nice possibilities," she said about the tall ceilings with their ornate molding.

"Great potential," she said of the hardwood floors.

"Modern plumbing," she noted of the kitchen. "Fas-cinating."

That was the last straw. He turned toward her and uttered one earthy, concise word.

"I wouldn't describe it as that bad," she countered.

"If you don't like it, get out."

"There are cables and camera equipment all over the place. Every room but the kitchen is sprayed with fake cobwebs and dust. The furniture looks like rejects from a Victorian nightmare. Is the upstairs this way too?"

"The furniture was brought in for the movie. Up-stairs is my domain. No one's allowed up there. Espe-cially you."

She sighed elaborately. "And thus, where is my room?"

"Behind the kitchen."

While she stared at his back in disbelief, he led her through the large, cheerful, amazingly *clean* kitchen to a tiny room with one window.

Caroline did a slow turn, taking in a twin-size metal bedstead and an ancient dresser.

"Is this the cook's room? Is she on vacation, or did she break parole and go back to the comforts of prison?"

"There's no cook."

Her gaze stopped on the floor fan that sat atop the dresser. "There's no air-conditioning!"

"Come back in five years. By then I might have a central unit installed."

"There's no phone!"

"Use the one in Frank's trailer." His blue gaze flick-ered down her body, pausing blatantly at her breasts and hips. "Since you and Frank are so close."

Caroline had been considering setting fire to the drab little room in protest. Now she considered setting fire to Dr. Belue. His insulting once-over made her skin feel hot enough to scorch his throat when she stran-gled him. She pivoted on one heel and faced him, then whipped her glasses off and stared straight into his eyes. "Are you insinuating something?"

Blue smiled wickedly. The madder he made this Beverly Hills bunny, the sooner she'd leave. "You look like the type who wouldn't have any scruples about married men."

Her eyes narrowed. He was only trying to provoke her. He wanted to get rid of her. She had to keep remembering that. Caroline scanned his naked chest and all the territory below it with nonchalant approval. "Ah, yes, married men are what I crave. Too bad you're single. Otherwise I'd seduce you."

"You'd walk bowlegged for a week afterward."

Caroline clasped a hand to her heart dramatically. She ignored the sensual loosening his words produced in her lower body. He was a volcano—unpredictable but fascinating. "How lovely. There must be dozens of bowlegged women around here."

"Hundreds."

"Hundreds of women with bad taste. Amazing."

"Hundreds of women with dazed smiles."

Caroline tsk-tsked, shaking her head. "You'll have to forgive me for ignoring an opportunity to join their ranks. Nothing personal. It's just that I prefer not to mate outside my species."

"And you wouldn't want to make Frank jealous."

Her grim amusement faded and her voice became somber. "Frank respects you. How can you accuse him of cheating on his wife?"

He didn't answer for a moment. Caroline felt bare as he looked deeply into her eyes.

"I'm not serious," he admitted finally. "I just don't understand why you took this job for him if you hate being here so much."

"He's been under a lot of pressure lately. Your manic-depressive wolf didn't help his stress level any. He's a good friend. He was almost my brother-in-law once upon a time."

"Hmmm. In a lucid moment Frank's brother realized his folly and broke the engagement?"

"He had severe diabetes. He died on his thirtieth birthday from a heart attack. Satisfied?"

He was silent for a moment, studying her shrewdly. "I apologize for doubting your sainthood."

"Spare me the alligator tears."

Her breath short, feeling a little light-headed from their intense conversation and her proximity to his half-naked body—didn't the man own a shirt?—she twisted back toward the room and swung out a disparaging hand. "I really must have a bedroom upstairs. Something bigger. With air-conditioning."

"You're out of luck unless you want to sleep with me."

"Perish the thought. I'd rather cuddle a tarantula."

"I can get you one. I'll leave it in your bed."

Goose bumps scattered down her spine. She could feel him still gazing at her. At the scar, undoubtedly. "Seen enough?" she demanded, shifting with anger.

"The scar, yes? I think it's interesting, yes. Dramatic. Not so ugly as you think."

Shaken by his frankness and insight, she blinked quickly and retorted, "I'm not self-conscious about it. I'm twenty-six years old and I've had the scar most of my life. You startled me earlier, that's all." *And for some insane reason, I wanted you to think I was beautiful*, she added silently.

"So why do you try to hide it?"

"So that rude boobs won't ask me how I got it."

"I've already failed the rude-boob test, *chère*. How did you get it?"

"Look, doc, I'm not desperate to share my life story with you. I'm probably the first woman you've met who can't be persuaded by your Cajun accent or your endearing little French terms. So cool the act."

"This is the way I always talk, *pichouette*. You're in Cajun territory now, and it's nothing like the rest of the world. Get used to it."

"Nothing like the rest of the world," she echoed tersely. "Just clannish and backward."

He grasped her forearms in a swift, angry attack, then lifted her to her tiptoes and stared down into her wide eyes. His expression was intense. "I'll put you out of my house if I hear that kind of insult again."

Her face pale, she pried his hands away and stepped back. "Apology offered. I'm not a snob. But just stay out of my way."

With trembling hands Caroline jerked her scarf off and flung it on the bed. "I claim this barren territory in the name of civilization."

She pointed to the door, giving him a stern look as she did. His eyes roamed over her hair and she knew it must be a crumpled mess from the scarf. Caroline resisted a near compulsive urge to straighten it. "Out, Dr. Dolittle," she ordered. "Go get my luggage and leave it by the door. Don't scratch it up. It cost a small fortune."

He frowned at her imperious tone and started to make a pithy comment, but someone called his name at the front door. "I'll be back," he told her tersely.

"I shall alert the media," she quipped in an English accent.

And the moment he got beyond the bedroom door, she slammed it.


Some people drank to forget their troubles, or ate too much, or developed other bad habits. Paul Belue played the accordion.

He sat on the edge of his bed in the moonlight,

squeezing a somber tune, his large fingers pressing gracefully into the enamel buttons that substituted for piano keys. His music, like his heritage, was all Cajun. The button accordion was a well-loved part of both.

*Dieu!* Caroline Fitzsimmons would keep him up all night figuring out his emotions. She was a bossy, conceited, quick-tempered hellion, and he didn't need to prove that he could tame that kind of woman.

He liked women; liked being friends with them, liked being nice to them and having them be nice in return. He was thirty-two years old and proud of the loving, long-term relationships he'd enjoyed thus far. There hadn't been hundreds of women, or even dozens. In fact, he could count the number on his fingers and have fingers left over. Quality not quantity was his motto.

Nothing in his life had prepared him for this she-devil.

He'd given her the worst room in the house when he could have offered her something comfortable upstairs. He'd taken cruel delight in baiting her today.

Then she had removed her glasses and turned her fierce, mesmerizing gaze on him. Her eyes were green around the edges with sharply etched, nearly black perimeters. Near the pupils they were gold. He'd seen such strangely colored eyes in animals, but never in a human before.

And her hair, *Dieu!* Even disheveled and mashed from hours under the scarf, it was glorious. Straight and thick, it hung to her shoulders in a blunt cut. It drooped over her left brow in a provocative, sultry way. The color was like blush wine or rose-tinted gold.

He found himself feeling sympathy for her as he had the first time he saw the scar. His insinuation about Frank had really hurt her; the pain was obvious in her eyes. She wasn't very good at hiding it. Perhaps that was another reason she favored sunglasses.

Now Paul uttered a few ugly descriptions of his own

vulnerability. It was foolish to feel softhearted toward such a silly, self-centered dame. She had marched out of her room tonight to eat dinner with Frank and some of the cast members, pointedly excluding him from an invitation. She had looked like some sort of desert queen in a sensual dress of pastel silks.

She stopped by the kitchen table, stared rudely at his bowl of red beans and rice, then ordered him to have Wolf waiting for her first thing in the morning. She rolled her eyes when he told her that he'd turned Wolf loose in the forests for a day or two, as therapy. Wolf would come back sometime tomorrow, maybe. She called him irresponsible for letting Wolf roam.

She left hurriedly when he threatened to dump her into a bayou.

Paul shut his eyes and concentrated on his music until an odd thumping noise interrupted him. He paused to listen, tilting his head to one side. The old mansion was full of strange noises made by benign ghosts. But ghosts didn't pound the ceiling downstairs.

He placed the location of the thumping and smiled broadly. The she-devil's sticky, hot bedroom. She was undoubtedly having trouble sleeping, and his music didn't help. She was sending him another of her orders: *Be quiet.*

Grinning, Paul played on, choosing a loud, raucous jig this time. Within a minute he heard footsteps on the long staircase to the second floor.

"Oh, no. Against the rules, *chère*," he muttered aloud.

Carrying the accordion, he strode to his door, flung it open, and went down a wide hall. She crested the top of the stairs and stopped in the pool of light from a wall sconce. He stopped in the shadows.

"Quit playing that thing, will you?" she asked. "It sounds like a dying moose."

Paul ignored her words and caught his breath at the smooth sensuality she radiated. Even in the dim light he could see her breasts moving swiftly against the thin material of her silky black pajamas. Her hair glistened with red and gold highlights. Her face was flushed with anger.

"I told you that upstairs is off limits to you Hollywood people," he reminded her. "Don't ever come up here again."

"You have window air conditioners in *three rooms up here*," she protested. "I walked around the house tonight and looked. "I want one of those rooms."

"No. Not upstairs. You're lucky that I let you stay downstairs." He squeezed the accordion for emphasis. It produced a short, squawking, somewhat indecent noise. "Get back where you belong."

"I'll go when you put that damned accordion down."

Smiling politely, Paul stepped into the light not more than five feet from her. He watched her eyes skim down his body. He watched them widen when she realized that he was wearing only the accordion, which he held at a crucial spot in front of him.

"Still want me to put it down, *chère*?" He pressed the accordion together slowly. It made a sound like a luscious sigh and revealed a good deal of his outer thighs and hips.

She lifted her chin and looked down her nose at him. She held her ground, he had to give her that.

"Oh, I see," she noted sardonically. "This is a sexual fetish peculiar to Cajuns. Pardon me."

He played several scales on the accordion, pressing and releasing it languidly between his large, sinewy hands while he gave her a lecherous smile. "Heh, heh, heh," he chortled. "Us Cajuns call this a squeeze box. You have anything as good?"

"Not with pleats in it." Looking unsettled, she grasped the front of her pajama top as if she were afraid he might burn it off with his gaze, then pivoted and stomped back downstairs.

Paul listened carefully until he heard her bedroom door slam shut. Then his rugged face contorted in discomfort. Reaching carefully between himself and the accordion, he began to disengage a thatch of curly black hair caught in the instrument's brass trim. He'd nearly crushed a hard part of his anatomy that desperately wanted to like Caroline Fitzsimmons, even when she was meddling and giving orders.

This woman was going to cause him pain in more ways than one.

Frank and the movie's director cranked up the cast and crew that day to shoot an outdoor scene that didn't require Wolf's presence.

Free to roam, Caroline investigated the plantation, meeting the staff and petting the animals. Ed invited her to play with the black-footed ferrets, a species that conservationists had barely rescued from extinction and were now trying to return safely to the wild.

She sat down in the middle of a large outdoor pen with a screened top, and immediately a dozen half-grown ferrets scampered over to her. Caroline laughed delightedly and spread her hands. *Come, babies. I won't hurt you.*

The ferrets climbed up her arms and stretched out on her legs. One hung from the back of her oversize tangerine-color blouse, and another draped himself over the crown of her voluminous yellow sunhat.

Laughing, the sunhat mashed around her face like a collapsed buttercup, she didn't notice when Paul walked up and gazed at her with astonishment.

This couldn't be the same glitzy babe who'd showed up in a limo yesterday, he thought. But yes—even covered in ferrets she looked chic, clean, and cool, untouched by human hands. Her blouse was orange; her flared shorts were yellow, like her sandals and the silly hat she wore and the scarf she'd twisted around her throat as a necklace. He could almost drink her; she was a tequila sunrise, sweet with a punch.

Paul rubbed a grimy hand across his sore jaw. What a punch. He listened to her soft, carefree laugh and wondered what kind of magic the animals wrought on her. He couldn't imagine her laughing like that around people.

She spotted him watching her, and her laughter faded. She lifted the brim of her hat, ferret and all, and squinted at him.

"You're filthy," she noted cheerfully, sweeping a jaunty gaze over his dusty jeans and T-shirt. His face and arms were streaked with dirt and sweat, and his hair was plastered to his head. She clucked her tongue in reproach. "Have you been wrestling with your conscience again?"

He was too tired to fight the she-cat, and the sound of her laughter had softened him in some way he didn't understand. He shrugged and smiled at her. "Been wrestling with an injured antelope."

"What happened to it?"

"Got its leg twisted in a fence. Tore ligaments. I operated on her a few days ago. She's not doing too well. We can't keep her off the leg without sedating her. If we sedate her, she won't eat or drink. Today we moved her into a smaller stall, where she'd be forced to rest." He paused, frowning distractedly at the scuff mark his work boot was making in the thick sawdust around the ferrets' cage. "She's one of only a dozen of her kind left in the world."

"Dr. Bluebeard, Frank said that you traded a fancy racehorse practice in New Orleans for this hard-luck life. Why?"

"Priorities, *chère*. The world has enough racehorses. It has enough doctors who want to take care of them." He gestured around him with one hand. "When I heard that this place was for sale in the parish where I grew up, I came back. It's where I belong."

"And you'll do anything to keep the place running. Even put up with a movie crew."

"You got it, orange blossom."

"Frank said your wolf was doing great, and then one morning he just refused to cooperate."

"He's not used to so many people, that's all." Paul grimaced in disgust. "One of the actors bit him on the ear."

"Kids can be—"

"Hell, I'm talking about the old guy who plays the hermit."

"Frederick?"

"He was supposed to whisper in Wolf's ear. In the script it says, 'Silver Wolf listens with great concentration.' Ol' Fred, he used to be on some soap opera or something and he says he would bite actresses on the ear to make them pay attention. Before I could stop him he bit Wolf."

"Oh, Lord. He bit a *wolf*? Did Wolf bite back?"

Paul looked proud. "Wolf's too well trained for that. No, he got revenge later, though. It was classic. *Bien!*"

She cocked one elbow and pantomimed a leg raising and lowering. Paul chuckled. "Exactly. Fred the fireplug."

They both laughed. Paul realized that he wasn't supposed to like her enough to laugh with her, and she seemed to have the same thought. They stopped awkwardly. She cleared her throat.

"How did Frank hear about you and Wolf?"

"One of the networks did a feature about the wildlife preserve here. Frank saw Wolf when I was being interviewed. When he came up with a script and movie deal, I didn't know how complicated it would make my life. I wish I didn't need the money."

Paul watched her pull the ferret off her hat and cup him in her arms, stroking his head. She was covered in the little animals, and they nuzzled her as if she were a long-lost friend. He'd never seen anything like it.

"What did you do?" he demanded, pointing at her. "Hide nuts in your clothes?"

She shrugged and looked away. "They probably just like my perfume or something."

"Ah. *Parfum de Nut.*"

She glanced at him and smiled, her head tilted to one side. Damn, the woman almost looked sweet.

"Can I see the antelope?" she asked abruptly.

That snapped him back to reality. "No. No visitors."

"I could help her, I'm sure."

He bristled at her self-confident words. "You have a degree in veterinary medicine, yes?"

"Medicine can only go so far, doc. I use massage on injured or tense animals. They like it just as much as humans do."

He stood hip-shot and leaned against the ferrets' cage, eyeing her sardonically. "You have a license to massage antelopes, yes? You have training?"

"I'm self-trained, doc. There aren't any schools for what I do."

"Let me guess. Mommy and Daddy bought you a liberal arts degree at college, and you couldn't get a real job with it."

"Wrong, doc. My parents died when I was five. I was adopted by my father's cousin and his wife. To put it mildly, we weren't the happiest family in the world, and I left home when I was seventeen. I never went to college." She hesitated. "I didn't even graduate from high school. But I'm damned good with animals. If you don't let me help your antelope, you're an idiot."

His curiosity over her turbulent background was lost in annoyance. Paul bowed with mock gallantry. "Your lack of charm is exceeded only by your bad temper."

Caroline watched him walk away and mentally rebuked herself for being so undiplomatic. He limped a little. Obviously the antelope had put up quite a battle with its three good legs. She told herself that she felt sorry for the antelope.

She left the ferrets' cage and went in search of Ed. She found him inside the plantation's aviary supervising two college interns in the feeding of baby birds.

"Quill sparrows," Ed explained. "Development in the Florida Everglades has almost destroyed them."

"Blue wants me to take a look at the injured antelope. He said you'd show me where she is."

"Sure."

An hour later Caroline walked out of the antelope's stall, smiling. Her subterfuge had been worth it. The delicate little creature was calmly curled up in a plush bed of straw, munching from a pile of alfalfa hay. Miss Antelope understood what Paul was trying to do for her now. She'd cooperate. Dr. Blue had better appreciate that fact.

Caroline frowned. Even the antelope had air-conditioning.

Thank goodness for moonlight. It turned his dark bedroom into sharply etched shadows. She found her way to the air-conditioner easily.

Caroline knelt beside the humming unit and glanced fearfully at the large bed where Paul lay under nothing but a white sheet. He made a disturbing sight—large, prime, and extremely masculine, sprawled on his stomach with the sheet pulled low on his back and one long leg angled out.

He was a wild man. He undoubtedly slept naked.

*Keep sleeping*, she urged silently as she took a second to scan his room. The furniture was antique, and sparse; old rugs covered the hardwood floor; the tall windows were covered with thin white curtains. A set of doors opened onto the back balcony.

His bedstead was a huge, ornately carved contraption set high off the floor. How regal, she thought, a majestic antique befitting a barbarian king. Her throat dry, she stared at his sleeping form for a long moment. She was treading in the barbarian's lair, and he was one savage beast who couldn't be soothed by the psychic music of her mind. That realization was wildly challenging.

Caroline turned quickly to the air conditioner. She latched a hand around its electrical cord and worked her way down to the plug. She wiggled the plug away from the wall outlet and held her breath as the unit went silent.

*Sweat, Dr. Doolittle,* she ordered grimly but silently.

A few determined sawing motions with a kitchen knife neatly cut the cord in two. Caroline tucked the severed end into the waistband of her pajama bottoms and stood up.

*Tiptoe like crazy,* her nerves urged. *Don't look back. Go!*

She had just reached the foot of the bed when his low, sinister voice floated off the pillow. "What do you think I should do in revenge, *chère*?"

Caroline jumped. The knife clattered to the floor. The cut electrical cord slithered down to the crotch of her pajamas. "Nothing, if you're smart," she answered as boldly as she could, considering that her knees were weak.

He turned over languidly, his broad torso looking very dark and imposing against the white sheets.

"Agree to give me an air-conditioned room and I'll apologize," she told him.

"You'll apologize anyway."

He swung his legs off the bed and tossed the sheet back. The moonlight covered him with teasing shadows, and he was definitely naked. He stood up and came around the corner of the bed toward her, his steps relaxed. He cleared his throat like a man just rising from a good night's sleep, ran a hand through his hair, then held out his hand palm up. He was close enough to touch her if he wanted.

"My cord," he demanded.

"My air conditioner," she countered.

The sudden explosion of movement caught her off guard. He leapt forward, snagged her around the waist with one arm, and anchored a hand in the neck of her pajama top. Caroline felt the button straining under his grip.

"I'll find my cord," he explained.

Then the button and all its fellow buttons went flying into the darkness. Her top hung open, baring a swathe of her naked skin to the room's cool air.

Caroline burst into action, stamping on his toes and swinging at him wildly. He grabbed her in both arms and pinned her against his body. "The cord, mademoiselle," he said calmly.

"Bastard! This is assault!"

"I'm holding you, not assaulting you. You're a trespasser. You're also a thief."

She grew still, her chest heaving with anxiety and the humiliation of being intimately clamped against his naked body. Her shirt had fallen back so that her breasts were against him, her nipples burrowing into his thick chest hair. His face was a mysterious shadow above her, but she could imagine the gleam of satisfaction in his eyes.

"Well, *chère*, at least I know where the cord is *not*. Let's see if it's down south." He rotated his hips against her slowly, and his growing hardness was unmistakable. "Ah! I feel something unique. Have you ever considered joining a freak show?"

"All right, you win," she whispered hoarsely, her body

burning. At the moment she wanted nothing more than to get away from the scent and heat of him. It was impossible to feel him against her and not want him. The thought was a basic admission of the sexual energy that had tinted every word, gesture, and look between them since the moment he'd opened the limousine's door.

She had known all along that she wanted him. She just hadn't known it so desperately.

"Take it out," he ordered. "Drop it on the floor."

Caroline swallowed harshly. Her nipples were stiff against his chest; his shallow breathing gave evidence that he felt the contact as much as she did.

"You mean the cord, I assume," she taunted.

"Anything else you find will be much bigger." His voice was a low rumble. "And it'll be connected to me."

"I'll be certain not to bother it."

"No bother."

She wedged her hand between their stomachs and worked it into her pajama bottoms. Caroline was so preoccupied with her mission that she leaned forward without noticing, and her forehead brushed the tip of his nose. She turned her face to one side, her breath rattling in her throat.

"Keep that thing out of my way," she muttered.

"Big nose, big . . ."

"Okay, okay, I believe the analogy."

Oh, how she believed it. The back of her hand pressed against him as she grasped the cord trapped between her thighs. She trembled and shut her eyes. Even more disastrous, *he* trembled.

"I don't know why I want you, you hellion," he whispered, "but I do." Despite his words his voice was gentle.

Caroline groaned. Trembling and gentleness were unfair weapons. She made her voice hard. "A little gratuitous sex, doc?"

"Shhh. I wouldn't take you to bed even if you asked me to."

Her head tilted back. She gazed up at him, open-mouthed. "That's the most arrogant thing I've ever heard in my life."

"Our circumstances don't make for much friendship, eh, *chère*?"

"Eh, no."

"Well, as much as I'd enjoy sharing my bed with you, I won't do it. I don't like to be used by strangers, no."

She was fascinated. It was either the best line in the world or she'd stumbled upon an incredible man. "I don't like to be used by strangers either," she murmured, her voice catching. "I've spent most of my life avoiding it."

"Poor Caroline." He brushed his lips across her scar.

The gesture was so disarming that a soft sound of anguish escaped from her throat.

"Poor Caroline," he whispered again, pulling her tighter against him.

With movements that made them both shiver again, she drew the electrical cord from her pajama bottoms and dropped it on the floor. "I don't want your pity," she said in a raspy voice. "I hate it."

"Shhh. So defensive." He nuzzled her face and kissed her on the mouth.

It was a slow, easy kiss, as erotic as the warm night and full of promise. But there were no promises between them. There were only differences, distances, and a past that she couldn't forget. Yet he was so incredibly desirable.

Tears slipped down her face even as she kissed him back, touching the tip of her tongue to his. Then choking sobs rose in her throat and she had to twist her mouth away in order to breathe.

He continued to hold her, his breath warm on her face while she cried with jerky little coughs.

"Maybe we could be friends, eh?" he offered by way of sympathy, and she heard the bewilderment in his voice. "We could try, yes?"

"No. Oh, n-no. We're safer as enemies." She pushed against his hold. "Let me go, Blue. I don't want anything to do with you."

He nearly released her, but his hand snaked around one wrist and kept her from backing away completely. He reached out and pulled her torn pajama top closed. Then he stroked her hair for a moment and ran his fingers over her scar.

"Don't touch it," she protested, whipping her head away.

"You're vulnerable there," he said gruffly. "It makes you feel helpless. But you confuse pity with compassion. Here. Feel."

He took her hand and drew it to the back of his neck. Caroline's fingers slipped across his warm, smooth skin until they reached a horrible swathe of raised tissue.

"Oh, God, Blue, so that's why you keep your hair long. What happened?"

"You tell me about yours, I'll tell you about mine." He glanced down at himself. "But first I'll cover the happy warrior here with a robe."

Caroline couldn't resist looking down too. Her eyes were attached to a willful part of her brain that had to see what she was going to miss.

She was going to miss quite a lot.

"No, don't," she said quickly, stepping farther away from him and fixing her gaze on his face. "I mean, I'm going back to my room. I really don't want to talk about my scar." She inhaled raggedly. "I don't want to be friends with you. It's too complicated."

"Life is simple at Grande Rivage, chère. You have only to give it a chance."

"No." Shaking her head almost desperately, she made a wide arc around him and headed to the door. She opened it and paused, looking back at him. He was a tall, inviting mixture of shadows.

"Get some sleep, *chère,*" he called. "Tomorrow I'll put an air conditioner in your window. Then you won't have to sneak into my room and pretend not to like me."

Strangling on self-rebuke for all the misery and confusion she'd brought on herself through a dumb prank, she stepped into the hallway and slammed his door shut.

# Three

Even a bad night's sleep didn't mar his enjoyment of dawn. Paul stretched widely and sucked quantities of cool, clean air into his lungs as he walked through the compound. Above the forest the eastern sky was splashed with Easter-egg colors.

He frowned, thinking about the emotional scene with Caroline, and his mood quieted. He could resist anything but the underlying gentleness in the she-cat's nature; he was drawn to the mysterious sorrow that made her so angry.

Shoving his hands into the pockets of the faded khaki trousers he wore, Paul strolled along lost in contemplation. Two of the female college interns yelled good morning to him from the window of the small white cabin they shared.

He raised a hand in reply and flashed a quick smile without really noticing them. He was vain enough to enjoy the way they ogled him as he walked past, but cynical enough to dismiss its importance. Superficial pleasures were easy to come by—and just as easy to forget.

When he rounded the corner of a building and saw

Caroline sitting on a small boulder in the panther's habitat, he forgot superficial pleasures and everything else.

Cursing under his breath, Paul ran to the tall chain-link fence that surrounded the habitat's wide moat. Within the circle of fence and dark water were two acres of woodland inhabited solely by a large, untamed, and entirely unpredictable cat as black as midnight and capable of killing any human who upset him.

The cat crouched at the base of the boulder where Caroline sat, his eyes fixed on her, the tip of his dark tail popping back and forth. She had her knees drawn up with her arms wrapped around them. She looked completely relaxed. She appeared to be talking to the panther.

Paul ran to a nearby building and retrieved a chunk of beef from a meat cooler there. Several fears tore at him: one involving a lawsuit from Caroline Fitzsimmons's relatives, one involving the loss of a new federal grant he needed badly, and the worst a mental image of what the cat's claws could do to her.

When he returned he unlocked the compound's gate and slipped inside, moving with a grace honed by years of delicate work with skittish animals. He walked up behind the boulder without her noticing, but the cat's yellow eyes turned slowly toward him.

Paul watched Caroline's back stiffen. "You don't have to sneak up on us, doc," she announced coldly.

Paul stopped, his teeth clenching, his fingers digging into the piece of meat he held in front of him. How did she know that he'd entered the habitat? "I'll deal with you in a minute," he answered. He advanced until the panther rose and gazed eagerly at the meat.

"Here you go, Cat," Paul murmured in a soothing tone, and tossed the chunk to him. Cat pounced on it, snatched it into his mouth, then galloped into the woods.

Caroline turned to eye him dourly. She propped her elbow on one knee and her chin on one hand. "Cat. Wolf. You don't waste energy on names, do you?"

Paul exhaled raggedly. She was out of danger—from Cat, at least. Her nonchalant stupidity enraged him. "*Tu es un peu zinzin sur les bords!*" he shouted. "Do you know what that means?"

Caroline's face paled. "No, and I certainly don't care to—"

"You're cracked around the edges! An idiot!"

"He wouldn't hurt me."

"How did you get in here?"

"I climbed the fence and waded the moat."

Paul swept a disbelieving gaze over her pristine outfit, a blue maillot with a print scarf wrapped around it like a skirt. "Float like a butterfly, sting like a bee," he muttered. "Talking is hopeless!"

He grabbed one of her wrists, pulled her forward, and scooped her over his shoulder. Hanging upside down, she clutched the back of his light tank top in silent shock as he marched out of the pen and slammed the gate.

He dumped her unceremoniously by the fence and backed her against the cool metal links. Her eyes were wide with amazement. He pointed a finger under her nose and said softly, his breath hissing against her face, "If I ever catch you in the pen with that panther again, I'll drag you to the main road and tie you to the mailbox, where you can wait for the next limousine to take you back where you belong."

Her gold-green eyes narrowed slowly until they became twin suns glowing behind her lashes. "The panther wouldn't have hurt me."

"How do you know that!"

*Checkmate.* She wasn't going to tell him or anyone else about her talent with animals. She'd learned from harsh experience that it was best kept a secret.

"Trust me . . ." she began.

"*Merde!* You think you can flounce around a full-grown panther as if it were some lazy house pet? Did you spend your formative years on drugs? What are you trying to prove, that you're a fool?"

Trembling from frustration and a disturbing sense of being very female in comparison to Paul's sheer masculine strength, she planted both hands against his chest and shoved him. He thrust his jaw forward belligerently and refused to move.

"Calm down and back off," she warned. "I know more about animals than you can learn in your whole life. You don't have to worry about me."

He made a derisive sound. She grabbed his face between her hands and pulled him to her. Caroline bit his lower lip and heard his muffled yelp of astonishment.

He anchored one hand on her jaw and held her still while he jerked his mouth away from her attack. His chest moving swiftly, he stared down at her through hooded eyes. "Play with fire, *chérie*," he said in a husky voice, "and you'll get burned."

She gasped as his arm snaked around her and pulled her forward and up so that she was standing on tiptoe, her torso mashed intimately against his. With only her blue maillot and his thin tank top between them, she felt as though her soft breasts were in direct contact with his hard-packed chest.

Caroline slid her fingers up his neck and wound them into his hair. "I'll pull out so much hair that you'll need a transplant."

His eyes glittered fiercely. "Are you pushing me away or pulling me closer?"

Caroline made a garbled sound of frustration. She wasn't certain at the moment.

He angled one of his legs between hers with a suddenness that caught her off guard. It destroyed her balance so that one foot dangled above the ground. She jerked on his hair reproachfully and tried not to wiggle atop his thigh.

"Is this how you want to become friends?" she asked tersely. "Friends don't humiliate each other."

"If we were friends you wouldn't try to scare the hell out of me," he retorted. "You wouldn't put yourself in a stupid situation where you could get hurt."

Caroline felt a pang of guilt. There was no way he could have thought anything but the worst of her, under the circumstances. He was frightened for her sake. He cared.

She was suddenly in serious danger of smiling widely, wrapping her arms around his neck in a hug, and thereby confirming his suspicion that she was nuts.

"I did a stupid thing. I'm honestly sorry," she blurted out.

He was so astonished by her apology that he just stared at her. "You're driving me crazy," he finally managed to say.

"Good. Now let me go. I'd rather not spend the entire morning straddling your leg."

At that his eyes became devilish and his smooth Cajun patois deepened, making him sound wicked and exotic. "Your body, she knows how to start a friendship better than you do, yes? Why are you squeezing me with your thighs?"

"I'm trying not to fall over!"

His voice dropped lower. "Oh, I won't let that happen, not before I do this."

He dipped his head, his eyes open and burning into hers as he started to kiss her. She was breathing so hard that she swayed in his powerful embrace. But she didn't push him away.

His mouth came down on hers, rough and hot. She moaned against the delicious assault and returned it.

The furry thing that shoved against their legs wasn't the least bit shy about intruding.

"What the . . . well, *bonjour!*" Paul exclaimed.

He drew back, frowning. Dazed, Caroline stared at him, her mouth open, her body still intimately astride his leg. Finally she followed his gaze downward. His arm loosened reluctantly. She hopped back, grasping the fence for support.

"You interrupted me," he told the newcomer, shaking his head in rebuke.

"You saved me," Caroline added drolly.

Slowly she sank to her heels. She stared into steel-gray eyes and temporarily forgot what had just happened between her and Paul. Caroline knew that she'd never met an animal as noble as the one who stared back at her now. "Hello, Wolf," she said politely.

Wolf tilted his head to one side, listening to the psychic greeting she conveyed also. He looked from her to Paul and back again. Then he plopped a paw on her shoulder and yipped softly, displaying the Labrador retriever hidden under his wild exterior.

"Well, I'll be damned," Paul muttered.

"Probably," Caroline assured him, but without true malice. She was caught up in Wolf's thoughts. The rush of communication was staggering, and his gleeful message unnerved her.

*Happy! Good! Master no more lonely! Master takes a mate!*

The atmosphere was electric in the aftermath of their tempestuous confrontation. Paul strode back to the house with Wolf at his heels, and she could tell that he was puzzled and annoyed by her effect on an animal he thought he understood completely.

Caroline, grinning, followed them through the house and into the kitchen. She sat down in a cane-bottom chair beside a massive, battle-scarred table that was little more than a slab of crudely finished timber atop legs as thick as her waist.

"I'll have Wolf wrapped around my little finger by the

end of the day," she announced. "He'll be fine. You'll see."

Without pausing to look at her, Paul uttered in French a one-word opinion of that claim. He slapped a coffee kettle under the sink faucet.

Caroline made a face at his well-formed back. "I don't care whether you believe me or not. And if you're going to insult me, do it in English. You're as American as I am."

"I'm Cajun, and proud of it. If you were Cajun, you'd understand."

She made an odd, strangled sound that was so plaintive, he glanced at her over his shoulder. Paul wanted to ask what was wrong, but he couldn't bring himself to forgive her for the panther incident, and for being so smug about Wolf, and especially for ruining his gallant intentions about women and friendship.

To hell with friendship. He wanted to chain Caroline Fitzsimmons to his bed, himself along with her, and see how long it would take for the two of them to scorch the sheets. Then they could discuss friendship.

"Swallow a bug?" he inquired.

She huffed in disgust. "You're so transparent. I may be demanding and cocky, but you admire that. Admit, it, Belue, you've met your match."

"Wolf likes you. Be happy with that."

"Wolf is smarter than his master. He's willing to give me a chance to do my job."

He turned around and shook the kettle at her. "You talk too much."

"Probably. I was an only child. It's a habit."

"Break it."

He busied himself at the stove. She ogled him shamelessly. He had a great rump, and the thin tank top didn't hide much of his magnificent back and shoulders.

This man would age well, adding a little more weight to his torso perhaps, but keeping the solid look of a boxer's physique. His shoulders moved fluidly, stirring his black hair where it brushed them.

His height and sturdy build fit the big table and oversize kitchen, she decided. His dark good looks made an intriguing contrast to the bright yellow floor tiles and white appliances.

The kitchen told her a lot about him. He looked comfortable, as if he spent a great deal of time there.

It was a plain but homey place, full of gourmet gadgets, many of them hanging from a wrought-iron rack over the stove. Cheerful yellow curtains covered a large window over the sink. Newspapers and science journals were scattered on the countertops.

A small cappuccino machine squatted on the counter that ran next to the refrigerator. Alongside the cappuccino machine sat a coffee grinder and glass canisters full of coffee beans.

"Dr. Blue, you're a confusing man," Caroline noted bluntly. "Practical and impractical at the same time. Your kitchen table looks like it was designed with a chain saw, what I saw of your beloved upstairs was spartan, and yet you indulge in gourmet kitchen toys."

"Don't talk to me," he ordered. He went to the refrigerator and began stacking breakfast items in his arms.

Caroline gazed hungrily at an uncut cantaloupe, a carton of eggs, and a chunk of cheese. "How kind of you," she said sweetly. "To cook for me."

"I'm not cooking for you. Go eat with Frank."

She should do that, she knew, but she rebelled at the thought of giving up Paul and Wolf's company.

"I can't," she told him. "I'm studying Wolf." That was true, at least. Wolf slumped on the floor, his dark gray head resting on his paws, his ears drooping.

After his momentary, misguided excitement over his master's new friend, he'd become melancholy again. "Is this typical?" she asked Paul.

"Yeah. He's been like that for a week."

Caroline propped her chin on one hand and gazed at Wolf, hoping to pick up information. But he was a blank. She sensed a deep sorrow within him, but couldn't pinpoint the source.

"After breakfast I'll give him a massage. Frank can plan to start using him again this afternoon."

Paul cracked eggs into an stoneware bowl with angry force. "Scrambled," he announced.

"Undoubtedly. Yum."

"Thought you were a knee-jerk vegetarian."

"A moderate. I eat chicken and seafood on occasion."

"How noble."

"I just don't like to eat anything that might have been a client. So far I haven't trained a hen or a fish." She sat down on the floor by Wolf and stroked his broad head. "I'll get you back to top form, sweetheart."

Wolf licked her hand. She glanced up and caught Paul watching them with chagrin. She stuck her tongue out at him and his expression darkened even more.

"All right, so Wolf likes you. But he's going to be more trouble than you expected."

"Everything here is more trouble than I expected. Complicated."

"No, *chère*, it's simple. I need Frank's money, so I'll put up with you. Wolf will snap out of his mood whether you work with him or not. You'll go back to Beverly Hills and leave me alone."

"Gladly," she muttered.

"It's nothing personal. I have a helluva workload around here, not enough help, not enough money, and the last thing I need is a complaining houseguest." Paul turned to face her and spread his arms in an encompassing gesture. "Simplicity. My life-style." He pointed to the cappuccino machine. "Simplicity makes small luxuries more enjoyable." He jabbed a finger at her. "Even you're simple." He swept a taunting gaze over her clingy blue maillot. "Easy to understand in all the important ways."

"Or so you'd like to think." Caroline leaned back warily and felt her heart pounding. He was remembering what had happened last night, and so was she.

"You've had the scar since you were a little girl. You hated it, so you became preoccupied with hiding behind an image. You're always on guard. Especially around men." He smiled knowingly, his eyes confident. "But let you get close to a lion tamer like me, and you purr."

Caroline kept a neutral gaze directly on him while her stomach shuddered from the fear that he was right. "I'll admit that we have a love-hate relationship." She tilted her head jauntily. "You love to think you're irresistible, and I hate to destroy your fantasy."

To her surprise, he chuckled, a low, sexy sound. Respect filtered into his eyes. "Be glad I don't feel like proving you wrong."

"Thank you kindly for the reprieve. I'll be too busy with Wolf to mope with disappointment. All I want is to finish this job and get as far away from magnolialand as I possibly can."

"Why do you dislike the South?"

She sighed grandly. "Sir, behind my sweet and innocent manner rests a story too tragic for words."

"Uh-huh. Sweet and innocent. Like a lady 'gator."

Caroline placed a hand over her heart and shut her eyes. "I shan't share it with a man of your sensitivity. It's too, too sad."

"Let's see. You had a Southern beau. He dumped you in favor of someone more docile, like maybe a Hell's Angel."

Caroline dead-panned, "And that broad wore the *tackiest* brass knuckles."

Paul stared at her in surprise. It was hard not to like a woman who could make fun of herself. It wasn't what he expected. They traded a look of tentative amusement until finally she coughed and looked away.

Paul noticed abruptly that her face was chalky. The color had begun to fade from her complexion when he'd asked why she didn't like the South.

"Do you feel all right?" he asked with more concern than he'd intended. "Does talking about this subject really upset you?"

Her eyes became wary at his gentle tone. "No. You're incredibly nosy."

"I'm always curious to learn about new forms of wildlife."

Paul picked up a dark red tomato from a wooden bowl by the sink. He leaned with deceptive laziness against the counter and bit into the tomato slowly, his eyes never leaving Caroline's.

His actions were so slyly seductive that she studied him in silent disbelief, her lips parted. She'd never seen anyone eat a tomato this way before. He delicately sucked the pulp into his mouth and licked juice from the palm of his hand, using just the tip of his tongue.

He took another bite—no, it wasn't so much a bite as it was a tugging motion that involved every inch of his lips. He didn't just eat the tomato, he enjoyed it.

Caroline felt a relaxed, damp sensation spread outward between her thighs. The man wanted her to imagine his lips on something besides a tomato, and he'd succeeded.

She stood up, straightened her fringed skirt with quick little jerks of her hands, and frowned at him. "That's indecent. And hardly original."

He nodded, his blue eyes crinkling merrily.

She scanned him from head to toe. "Your weapons are grand, doc, but this is one warrior who's seen it all before. Tomatoes are overrated. So is sex. I'll eat with the movie crew. Have Wolf at Frank's trailer in forty-five minutes."

She turned on one heel and walked out of the kitchen. For the first time since they'd met, she heard him laugh, really laugh, as if he were having a fine time. It was a hearty, wonderful sound, and the only thing that made her teeth grind was the realization that he was laughing at her.

Wolf was like putty. She couldn't penetrate the privacy of his mind, but she knew he loved having a massage. He lay on his side on the floor of Frank's trailer, taking up all the walking room, his eyes closed blissfully. He weighed close to two hundred pounds and was at least six feet long from nose to tip of tail.

"So give me some background on the beast," Caroline told Frank, who sat on a couch nursing a glass of Perrier and antacid.

"Wolf? Well, in the movie he—"

"Not Wolf-beast. Dr. Belue-beast," Caroline corrected him. "Since you and he seem to be friends, I thought you could tell me about him."

"Oh. What do you want to know?"

"Was he born around here or did he just crawl out of the swamp fully grown?"

Frank smiled. "His family settled this land more than two hundred years ago, when the British drove the French Acadians out of Canada. A ne'er-do-well ancestor lost the land to a rice planter in a card game. The planter built the mansion, but that glorious avenue of oak trees that leads to it was planted by the first Belue owner. Paul grew up not far from here, on the coast, where his family fished for a living. After he worked in New Orleans as an equine specialist for a few years, he came back home. I think he bought a couple thousand acres."

"Not many Cajuns have that kind of money. Even a veterinarian."

"He and his brothers were ambitious."

"Big family?" She said the words sarcastically, to hide her envy.

"Yes. Five kids. Pretty scattered now, I understand. But very loving. Anyhow, when Paul was a teenager they found oil on a little strip of land they owned. Before oil prices went bust, they made a small fortune. Paul used his part to go to vet school. Like I mentioned the other day, he built up a pretty nice practice in New Orleans working with Thoroughbreds at the tracks. Gave it all up a couple of years ago to come down here and save the endangered whatever."

Caroline frowned thoughtfully. "He's dedicated. It's obvious."

"This place is his life. He nearly kills himself trying to keep it going. If he acts like a pain, it's because he's worried about it."

"Hmmm." Caroline's fingers slid under Wolf's thick hair and stroked his neck. "Wolf adores him." Plus the panther had shown respect when Paul came in his pen that morning, and the respect was genuine, not based on fear.

She was impressed with the quality of care all the animals received. He cared for them and about them.

"So are you ready to make friends with Paul?" Frank asked hopefully.

Friendship was certainly an important issue in her life lately, she thought. Caroline shook her head. It had never sounded so dangerous.


Caroline pushed a pair of blue-rimmed sunglasses higher on her perspiring nose and watched Dabney—no last name, just Dabney, for reasons of creative impact—hiss her way through a scene inside the mansion's main study.

Music connoisseurs under the age of eighteen had

made her a minor rock star. She looked like a young female Elvis in a leather miniskirt. In *The Legend of Silver Wolf,* Dabney played a villainess.

Elvis was probably spinning in his grave, Caroline decided.

"I want the map for the gold, you little brat," Dabney told Toddy, a cute redhead who'd first made his name in bologna commercials.

Toddy, looking frightened but determined, just as the script demanded, wound his little hand into Wolf's ruff. "No."

In the tense silence that followed, Wolf looked up at Dabney with all the animation of a rock. Caroline winced. "Growl at her, dammit," the director commanded, clutching her punkish orange hair in distress. "This is the fifth take."

Caroline stood slightly behind Paul and to his right, where she could be effective but unnoticed. "Speak, Wolf," he ordered.

Caroline closed her eyes and concentrated. *Please, Wolf. For Paul's sake.*

"Urrf," Wolf offered without enthusiasm.

Groans of dismay rose in the room. "Cut," the director said in disgust.

"Well, at least he's progressing," Frank noted, rubbing his temples. "He made a sound."

Toddy's mother stormed onto the set like a large red-combed hen and grabbed her son's hand. "We're going to our trailer and channel for a while, and try to get some insight from our spirit guides," she announced. "Toddy can't deal with these delays. The wolf is brain-damaged."

"Lunch, one hour," the assistant director called.

Paul walked to Wolf and knelt down beside him. Caroline followed. Wolf looked from Paul to her mournfully. *Sad. Friend hurts. I hurt. Sad.*

Caroline inhaled sharply and removed her sunglasses

so that she could look at him closer. *What friend, Wolf?*

*She-friend.*

*I'll help. Show me.*

*Gone now. Hope she come back.* Wolf cocked his head to one side and lifted his ears. *You help?*

*Yes.*

"The secret is your eyes," Paul interjected brusquely.

Caroline glanced over and found him staring at her almost as intensely as Wolf was. "Pardon?"

"Your eyes are unusual. Animals are fascinated by them."

She blinked rapidly, uncomfortable under his scrutiny. "That must be why you're so intrigued."

He made a gruff sound of amusement. "Yeah." Then he pointed to Wolf and asked dryly, "Got him wound around your little finger yet?"

"Ye of little faith, shut up."

He stroked Wolf under the chin. "It's okay, *mon ami.* You'll get it right the next time. Don't pay any attention to Toddy's mother. Let her go talk to her spirit guides. When she channels, she probably picks up reruns of *The Gong Show.*"

Caroline looked at Paul in wonder. She had expected him to rebuke Wolf, who was jeopardizing a lucrative project. Instead, this stressed-out, overworked, brusque tower of a man stroked Wolf's head as if he were a sick puppy.

Her heart melted into a puddle. "He's doing better," Caroline said softly, her eyes never leaving Paul. "He's concentrating more than before."

"Yes, he is." Paul gave her a reassessing look and nodded. "You helped. I don't understand how, but you did."

She was probably making a mistake, but she didn't care. "Let's go someplace private with him and eat lunch."

"Oh, ho, you'll put up with my company to help Wolf, yes?"

"I'm a martyr."

He ran a hand through his hair, and she watched the way the black strands gleamed under the set lights. She'd never cared for longish hair on men, but on him it seemed appropriate. One didn't clip the mane on a wild stallion.

"All right, let's go." There was something sly about the sideways look he gave her. "We'll catch our lunch."

"Oh, no. Lead me to a garden and I'll corner some lettuce, but I'm not going to—"

"Worthless, pampered—"

"Domineering, uncivilized—"

"Hi, Paul," Dabney interjected smoothly. "Hi, uhm, Casey."

Caroline squinted up at the actress. "It's Caroline."

"Right." Dabney smiled at Paul. "I just wondered if you wanted to eat lunch with me again. I'm going to watch music videos in my trailer."

"We've already made plans to kill our lunch," Caroline explained.

The girl eyed her quizzically. "Excuse me?"

Paul stood, took Dabney's hand, bent over it gallantly, and kissed her fingertips. "I'm sorry, but I have too much work to do, *petite*. Believe me, though, it's hard to turn you down."

"Hmmm. Okay, babe. I'll be waiting."

Caroline rose casually, fiddling with her sunglasses as if they required all her attention.

"You're the dog person, right?" Dabney asked her.

"Animal trainer," Caroline corrected the young woman.

Dabney studied her from under a tornado of black hair. "Oh, yeah. Listen, I want to ask you something. I'm real blunt, so don't be offended."

"Oh, I don't offend easily." Out of the corner of her eye she saw Paul arch one brow in disagreement.

"Well, it's just that . . . why don't you do something about that scar? I could recommend a great plastic surgeon."

Caroline stared at her for a moment. *Eat hot death, songbird.* "No, I like it. Men think it's sexy. Sometimes I wear a patch over the eye next to it. The mystery drives guys wild."

"You've gotta be kidding."

"Try wearing a patch. You'll see. The sympathy factor alone is worth it."

Startled, Dabney stared at her. "Unreal."

"Absolutely not."

Wolf picked up on her silent distress. He moved abruptly, bumping Dabney so hard that she stumbled backward. He effectively wedged himself in front of Caroline. Then he looked up at Dabney and bared his teeth.

"Wolf, no," Paul said in surprise.

Dabney's eyes widened in alarm. "What'd I do?"

Caroline patted Wolf's head. "I think it's just your perfume. He's sensitive to odd odors. Come on, Wolf, let's get some fresh air." She walked out of the room with Wolf beside her.

In the kitchen Caroline grabbed a glass of water to disguise her shaking hands. She was used to comments like Dabney's. Girls who based their careers on their looks were morbidly curious about the scar. But she wasn't used to having Paul Belue around to enjoy her embarrassment.

He ambled into the kitchen, his thumbs latched in the pockets of his khaki trousers. He sat down on the table, his booted feet swinging nonchalantly, and grinned at her.

"Nice technique," he offered.

"I hope she's smart enough to be insulted."

"She deserved it."

"Interesting taste in women you've got there, doc.

How old is she? Twenty, twenty-one? Maybe Wolf just has too much class to work for you anymore."

"Thanks, Mom, for the lecture."

"You're welcome. No wonder you weren't desperate to take me to bed. You're diddling a female Elvis impersonator. How intriguing." Caroline put the glass down, adjusted her skirt, and glanced at him coolly.

Paul chuckled. "When I diddle someone around here, you'll be the first to know, *chère*." He pointed upward. "Just listen for my bed bumping the wall."

"Anything would be better than listening to your accordion." She scowled. "Enjoy my scar story?"

"Hey," he said softly. "You've got guts. It must not be easy to put up with helpful advice, especially from a kid like Dabney."

She shrugged. Then, spurred by a sense of trust that perturbed her, she grew very still and looked at him with quiet dignity. Caroline gestured toward her scar. "This is as good as it gets—at least until medical science advances a little more. The doctors took care of the smaller scars, and I'm just grateful my face turned out as well as it did."

Slowly, compassion softened his eyes. "How bad were you hurt?"

"Well, let's put it this way—I didn't need a Halloween mask when I was growing up."

Abruptly he rose, came over to her, and cupped her chin in one hand. "How did it happen, *chère*?"

The feel of his thick, warm fingertips on the tender underside of her jaw made rivulets of sensation trail down her body. His low, soothing voice with its French accent was utterly disarming. No wonder animals liked him. She realized that she was leaning toward him, her lips parted.

And he was a reminder of everything she wanted to forget about her past.

Caroline pulled away, tossed him a sardonic look,

and put all her defenses back in place. "Forget it. I hate sentimentality. Let's go kill something for lunch."

He tilted his head to one side and gazed at her intensely, his eyes burning into her. After several awkward seconds in which she felt like a butterfly pinned to the floor, she shook both fists at him and yelled, "Dammit, what do you want?"

He blinked as if trying to remember. Then his eyes narrowed to wicked slits and he smiled. "Crawfish, *chère*. Crawfish."


They looked like tiny little ugly lobsters, and they were determined to humiliate her.

"No, Caroline, shoo them, don't scatter them," Paul ordered in a loud, exasperated voice. He dipped a tightly meshed net into the water once again, waiting. Wolf lay upstream on a sandy bank, watching them with what amounted to a wolf smile.

Caroline hopped. "They keep scooting over my toes! How do I know they won't pinch me?"

"A mudbug can't hurt you."

Wading barefoot in the shallow creek, she shuffled around, muttering. "I walked a half mile into the woods to herd crawfish. This is what I've sunk to. A shepherdess for low-rent shrimp." Her voice rose. "Mudbug? I'm not eating anything with a nickname that includes the word *mud*."

"Here they come! Yes, I'd run from such a woman too! Better to be eaten than nagged to death." Paul lifted the net swiftly. It was full of crawfish. "Lunch!"

Caroline picked her way across the streambed to him. She put one foot down on a harmless-looking rock. It was covered in a slick coat of algae.

"Help!" She came very close to doing a split.

Paul reached out to grab her. He made a chortling sound of amusement until her outflung hand caught his left knee. His foot went out from under him on the glassy rocks, and he sat down heavily.

Crawfish flew everywhere. Caroline fell sideways and ended up with her head in Paul's lap. She wore her hair in a jaunty topknot. A tiny crawfish latched onto the end of it and swung gently to and fro by her ear. His relatives disappeared into the creek.

"I don't like Cajun food anyway," she muttered, and added several choice words hot enough to boil their escaped lunch.

"*Dieu!* You're ridiculous!" Paul told her, his face red with restrained laughter. His gaze went to her white necklace, then to the outline of her breasts in the wet maillot. "Your baubles have sand on them. But I like sandy baubles. I should keep you around just for entertainment."

She pushed herself up from his flat, muscle-terraced stomach, staggered to the bank, and sat down. Paul was highly impressed by the fact that she ignored the crawfish still dangling from her hair. She untied the scarf around her waist and wrung water from it.

"This cost two hundred dollars. I don't think it's creek-wash and wear."

"What a useless way to spend money."

He stood, pulled his tank top off, and tossed it on a low bush. His unbelted trousers hung low on his hips. Caroline tried to give him no more than a baleful glance, but her hands twisted the scarf with increasing tension. If Dr. Blue had indeed risen full-grown from the swamp, the swamp had done a fine job creating his essentials.

"Cut the self-righteous attitude," she said in a strained voice. "You're just like everyone else. If you had the money, you'd buy all sorts of frivolous things."

He stretched on his side next to her, looking languid but poised in a way that reminded her of the panther. Before she could stop him he reached out and deftly removed the crawfish from her hair, then tickled it along her cheek before he tossed it into the creek. The warmth of his hand and the scent of his skin lingered like a caress.

"Maybe," he admitted. "But I wouldn't build my life around them. We Cajuns know what's important."

Caroline flung the scarf into her lap. "Being Cajun isn't the most wonderful claim in the world," she told him, her voice low and fierce. "Despite the fact that the media has made it into something romantic. There's nothing romantic about your damned heritage, and I'm tired of hearing you brag."

His cold blue eyes warned her to watch her step. "How did you get so prejudiced and small-minded?"

After a moment of silence she sighed as if she'd just made a painful decision. "My mother was Cajun." Caroline pointed to her scar. "She's responsible for this."

# *Four*

He couldn't have been more stunned if she'd told him that her mother came from the moon.

Paul sat up slowly, studying her, watching her jaw flex with emotion and her cheeks flush darkly, making the scar stand out like a vivid white brand. She stared down at her wet scarf and began wringing it again while her lips pressed tight in a line of defense.

Now he understood her infinitely better—the private look in her eyes, the reserve that kept her a little separate from other people, the jaunty anger, and the vulnerable underside that made her put up a shield.

"Michelle Ancelet," she said suddenly, her voice grim. "That was her maiden name."

"What parish was she from?"

"I don't know. I never tried to learn anything about her."

"You know enough to hate her, *chère*. Where did you learn that?"

He calmly absorbed the sharp look she flung at him.

"I don't hate her. I'd have to remember her to do that, and the accident wiped out my memories. Anyway, I was only five when it happened."

Caroline paused, and he watched the subtle shifting of sorrow and disgust across her face. A killdeer startled her with its loud, ringing call from a nearby marsh, and she hugged herself as though the sound hurt.

"Caroline," he said gently, "how much *do* you know about your parents?"

"My father was a regular *Américain,* as you Cajuns call them. John Fitzsimmons." She looked down her nose with mock grandeur and added in a haughty tone, "Of the Connecticut Fitzsimmons. He was an engineer."

"And how did a Connecticut Yankee end up in King Arthur's swamp?"

"I've been told that during college my father had a roommate from New Orleans. Dear Old Dad visited his roommate's home a few times, loved the city, and came back after college to live there."

"And so, your mother?"

"Came from a Cajun farm family, worked in a food-processing plant in New Orleans, and met my father when he was hired to redesign the plant."

The delicate distaste in Caroline's voice annoyed him. "Vegetable chopping is honest work," Paul told her.

To his surprise, she nodded. "I wouldn't care if my mother had danced naked with a stalk of broccoli if she were a good person. But she wasn't.

"She was looking for a way out of her situation. She was very pretty and exotic, and apparently my father was a shy, awkward, and not particularly handsome man who thought he'd died and gone to heaven when she showed some interest in him."

"Who told you all this?"

"His cousin. My stepfather."

"Give me more," Paul urged, scooping his hands toward his chest with great impatience, eager to pull the information out of her realm and into his.

Her eyes widened at his attitude. "Why do you care so much, doc?"

"More!"

"All right!"

She squirmed and eyed him warily, but the expectant way she bit her lower lip told him that she was glad to unload her past on a good listener. Poor Caroline, he thought sadly. How few people had ever heard this story?

"None of my father's family knew about her until Dad announced that he'd gotten married. He brought his new bride to Connecticut and introduced her."

Her voice became sardonic. "She couldn't read or write—to the intellectual Fitzsimmonses I'm sure she must have seemed like a bad joke. She caused some kind of embarrassing row with my grandmother Fitzsimmons over the treatment of a pet cat—the story goes that she called Grandmother several choice names for having the cat put to sleep. And last but not least, she was a chronic flirt and she tried to seduce my uncle."

Paul frowned. "And you think that's all true?"

Caroline smiled grimly. "I don't know. I'll give my mother one credit—she was right to hate Grandmother."

"Don't you have any respect for your *grand-mère*?"

She shot him a piercing glance. "You loved your grandparents?"

"Yeah."

"Respected them?"

"Yeah."

"Good. I envy you. Grandmother Fitzsimmons was the only one of my grandparents I ever knew. One Christmas she gave her other granddaughters porcelain dolls in full Victorian dress. I got a stuffed bear with that cheap, slick polyester fur that melts when you get it too close to heat."

Caroline paused. "I tested it. I burned the damned thing."

Paul grimaced with sorrow for her. "Hey, I shouldn't have—"

"My grandmother Fitzsimmons liked to pinch blue marks on my arms and tell me how glad she was that my face was so ugly—that way I couldn't cause the same kind of trouble my mother had. She said God was making me suffer for what my mother did."

Paul stared at her in silent, sympathetic horror. His reaction made Caroline look away quickly, swallowing hard.

"You see," she added in a hoarse tone, "it didn't help that I was born only five months after the wedding." She glared at him meaningfully. "And I was *not* premature." Wilting a little, she clasped her hands in her lap and slumped. "So I was probably the only reason for the marriage. Everyone, dear Mom and Dad included, must have really been thrilled about me right from the start."

He reached out and brushed the backs of his fingers across her scar, the gesture soothing. She didn't pull away as she had the night before. This time her eyes flickered with a gratitude that seared him to the core. Paul withdrew his hand slowly. She probably wouldn't admit it for some time yet, but she wanted every ounce of friendship he had to offer.

Friendship, not just sex. The former was much more difficult, and he'd have to work fast before she traipsed back to California.

"The accident," he said simply.

She took a deep breath, then exhaled with weary resignation. "Pit bulls have less tenacity than you do."

He chuckled. "Yeah."

Her gaze held his. "She and my father had a lot of problems. Even with plenty of money and a big house in New Orleans, she wasn't content."

"This is what you remember?"

"No, this is what I've been told. I have only flashes of memory from that period, nothing concrete."

"Hmmm."

"She had a lover. A Cajun."

"Of course. We Cajuns are all bad." He said the words sardonically.

"Now look, Dr. Blue, this is the truth about my past. You wanted to know."

"The truth you've been told might not be true at all."

She drew back angrily, like a cat about to arch its back and spit. "No one from the Ancelet family ever cared to offer a different version!"

"Keep going, don't argue," he ordered, waving her anger away impatiently. "Tell me all these rumors you were given."

Breathing hard, staring at him furiously, she gathered steam like an overworked engine, which was what he'd hoped she'd do. He wanted to get everything out in the open before she realized how much she was revealing about herself and retreated.

Her voice rose. "My mother deserted my father and took me with her."

Caroline stood up, walked a few feet away, and stood with her back to him. "She took me to live with her parents. My father went after her. There was a big fight, she got drunk, she and I left in a car, and he followed. A few minutes later she lost control and the car ran headfirst into a tractor-trailer rig. Mother was thrown out of the car and killed. I went through the windshield."

*"Dieu!"*

Paul got up and reached for her, but she moved away, bitter with the world now. She clutched her wadded scarf to her stomach, whipped around to face him, and planted her bare feet solidly in the deep sand.

"My father found the accident. That night, while I was in surgery, he shot himself."

Even his worst imaginings hadn't prepared him for this. Stunned, Paul stared at her open-mouthed.

Her anger deflated and she looked as if she might crumple. "He didn't even care that his daughter was alive and needed him. He just didn't care. See? Those are my memories. Those are what ate at me the whole time I was growing up. I can barely stand to be back in Louisiana."

"Caroline, shhh." He held his hands out, cajoling her with body language because he didn't have adequate words.

"It appears that after I got out of the hospital no one in my mother's family wanted me. None of the noble Cajuns wanted a hideous little mangled girl. So I got stuck with my father's cousin and his wife in Connecticut, who never let me forget how much trouble I was and how grateful I ought to be that my father's family, at least, was decent!"

Paul moved toward her, crooning a soft, deep sound in the back of his throat.

She looked at him in alarm. "Stay back! I don't want sympathy from you or anyone else around here!"

The broken, pleading quality of her voice told him that she didn't know what she wanted, except to figure out how people could be so rotten to their own flesh and blood.

"That's okay, I understand," he murmured as he reached her. Then he swept one arm around her shoulder and the other around her waist.

Her mouth popped open and she dropped her lump of scarf. He pulled her against his half-clothed body and cuddled her in a bear hug that was too kind and soothing for her to resist.

"We're capable of lots of *good* things too, us Cajuns," he told her in a very low voice. "Like this, see?"

She shivered, covered her face with both hands, and stood rigidly within his grasp while he talked to her softly, telling her that he understood why she felt the way she did, telling her that it was all right for her to take it out on him, that he didn't mind.

When he said that, she sagged against him like a broken doll, digging her hands into his arms while she bowed her forehead to his shoulder. "I'm sorry for taking it out on you," she offered in a tearful voice. "My feelings are nothing personal against you, Blue."

"You think all Cajun women are like your mother? I take that personal."

"That's not what I meant. It's just that I've spent my whole life hating her and my father for the mess they made of their lives and mine. I didn't deserve to suffer for their mistakes."

"You're right, *chère*, you're right." He rubbed one big hand up and down her back, massaging the tense muscles there. The wind brushed through the trees around them, showering them with leaves. One fluttered into her hair and he carefully removed it, then stroked the hair back into place.

Paul frowned, thinking of ways to reason with her. "My father, he was a fisherman, okay? Couldn't read or write. Neither could my mother. We lived in a lousy little frame house with a rusty tin roof."

He chuckled. "But that was one clean and neat lousy little frame house. My folks worked hard, and they were honest. I have four fine brothers. We had good food, good music, friends, church, community—very strong."

Paul held her a little tighter. "So don't hate the whole barrel of apples because one was rotten."

She groaned into his shoulder. "I know. It's wrong." She looked up at him regretfully. "I just don't belong here. The sooner I get through with this job and go back to California, the better."

Paul cradled the back of her head in his hand and looked down at her silently. With her gold and green eyes so close, so sad, and her hands laying against his chest trustfully, she showed a side of herself that drained him of rational thought and made his heart hammer in his chest.

After what she'd just shared with him, he knew that he'd completely misjudged her character. This woman had whipped dragons all her life, and there was nothing pampered about her. The knowledge quickly aroused him.

"You're quite a lady," he whispered.

She tilted her head to one side in surprise. With her bobbing topknot of hair, she reminded him of a sad, curious poodle. He smiled.

She gave a mildly annoyed sigh but admitted, "I like your smile even when you're making fun of me. Maybe we could strike a truce until I go home."

"*Bien.* I like your smile too. Maybe I can provoke it more often." He shifted against her, trying politely to move his blatant stiffness out of the way.

Too late. Her lashes flickered as she glanced down at their melded torsos. "That doesn't make me smile, doc," she said in an awkward tone, the color rising in her face. "Although it definitely would if I planned to stay around here, which I don't."

He clucked his tongue in mild reprimand. "Here I'm being a gentleman, and you complain." Paul finally managed to twist his torso so that his arousal no longer indented her stomach, but he felt her heart racing against his chest and knew that her resistance was a desperate facade.

"Is that a sigh of relief I heard, doc?"

"Nah, *chère,* it was your own sigh of disappointment."

They gave each other looks that quickly became strangled with repressed smiles of pure naughtiness. He arched a black brow at her. "Now that we're friends, how about I introduce you to a few local treasures?" He cut his eyes with comic lechery.

From the intense way she gazed up at him, her eyes half shut, her mouth half open, as if she wanted to be kissed—could the she-devil read his mind?—Paul knew that he had a very good chance of convincing her to go along with his offer.

"What treasures?" she asked softly.

"Cajun things." He rubbed circles in the curve of her spine, letting his fingertips explore the territory of bone and muscle so that she had to know that he was making a map in his mind. Paul felt her quiver under his touch.

She tossed a disapproving look toward the creek. "Will we have as much fun as today?"

"Better than that. We'll go eat some Cajun food tonight and do some dancing."

She looked skeptical.

"You know so little about your mother's people," he reminded her. "Be fair. I have a feeling that you want to be fair with people if they'll be fair too."

She nodded, her eyes flickering with admiration for his insight. "It's all I ask."

On impulse he kissed the tip of her nose. When he drew back, her eyes shone with emotion. She blinked, squinted at him shrewdly, and asked in a firm voice, "I won't have to catch my dinner, will I?"

He laughed heartily. She bit her lip, smiled, then laughed a little with him. It was the first time he'd heard her laugh, really laugh, other than when she was with the ferrets. Wanting to absorb the sound, he struggled not to kiss her.

From the general direction of the plantation came the honking of a car horn. She lifted her wrist and gazed at the wide ceramic bracelet that contained an elegant watch face. "So much for lunch. The crew must be signaling us. We're late."

Paul slowly unwound his arms and noted that she didn't leave too quickly. She became very formal and busily straightened her wet, wrinkled scarf, but she stayed close to him. He smiled to himself.

"*Chère?*"

"Yes?"

"You make pretty good mudbug bait."

She threw the scarf at his head.

After lunch Wolf growled heartily and on cue for the scene that had caused so much trouble that morning, and now he went through his paces in the outdoor scene as if he were the only calm creature within a hundred miles.

Caroline stood on the sidelines, sipping a diet drink and peering out from under a sunhat contentedly.

Wolf looked over to confirm her promise from time to time. *You help, she-friend?*

*I'll help.*

He went back to work with a vigor that made Paul whoop with pleasure.

Caroline was happy to make Paul happy—she was willing to admit that. She felt as if some strange power had taken hold of her; she'd never intended to tell him her melodramatic history, or huddle in his arms like a sad child, or let him talk her into going out with him.

Their lunchtime encounter had left her drained and yet revitalized. She frowned, trying to categorize the odd feeling. It was something like the sensation she got after an hour of exercising with her Jane Fonda videos.

She'd read somewhere that the pleasant exhaustion from aerobics was nearly as good as the languor that followed great sex. Good grief—what did that reveal about her feelings for Blue? Having never had great sex, she could only speculate.

Frank's brother, Tom, had been the sweetest, most unselfishly loving man she'd ever known, and he'd melted a lot of her defensiveness. Caroline smiled pensively. Thanks to Tom, she'd become a much nicer person.

But by the time she met him, severe diabetes had taken a toll on his energy. Still, they enjoyed a beautiful relationship and it made her regret the callous way she'd treated men before.

Not that she'd known any mature, sensitive men before she met Tom. She was a loner; she remembered only the crude, demanding boys from high school.

She'd dated the bad guys, the troublemakers, boys who worried her stepparents to no end, exactly as she wanted. Revenge had been more important than self-respect.

Caroline watched Paul guide Wolf through a few more rehearsals of the current scene. Paul Belue, hmmm. Here was a man who didn't fit either of the extremes she'd experienced with the male of the species. He was sweet but lusty, gentle but wild.

Caroline realized that just thinking about gentle, lusty, sweet, wild Paul Belue was enough to make hot sensations slip down the inside of her belly like melted sugar. She shut her eyes and desperately willed him out of her thoughts.

Wolf's sharp excitement plunged into her mind. Caroline jerked her eyes open and stared at Wolf, who stared beyond the barricade of lights, camera equipment, and people toward some impending disaster.

"Waaatch out!" Ed Thompson called from somewhere near the pastures. "Gaaate ooopen! Llamas ouuut!"

Chaos.

Dabney, lounging in the director's chair with her black miniskirt hiked to the tops of her thighs, leapt up screaming and ran around like an addled blackbird. Crew members climbed onto anything available. Frank came out of his trailer, grasped his head in horror, and simply stared.

Dozens of llamas overran the set.

Caroline began to chuckle. These long-necked, big-eyed darlings were as dangerous as a patch of petunias. They stopped amid the equipment and people, their funny little heads turning to and fro in curiosity, their shaggy sides heaving with exertion.

Paul strode into the middle of the set, where Dabney was surrounded like Custer at the Little Bighorn. She dodged the llama's snuffling noses.

"They won't hurt anyone," Paul announced.

"They're biting me!" Dabney squealed, and latched on to him with both hands.

The llamas were indeed smooching her with their mobile, soft, little mouths. "They're just friendly, *petite*," Paul told her, but he gazed at the llamas in consternation.

She cringed—the llamas were now tugging at her tangled black hair—and threw both arms around him. Caroline tapped one foot impatiently and frowned at the scene. Ed and several college students finally arrived and began scattering the invaders.

But the llamas weren't finished with Dabney. They began to spit at her, rotating their mouths like old men with lips full of snuff, then nailing her with uncanny accuracy.

The crew hooted. People clasped their stomachs and fell off their safe perches. Even Frank bent his head to the door frame of his trailer and laughed until he went weak-kneed and had to sit down. Caroline watched with a giddy smile. Wolf flopped by her right foot and made long, exuberant *roooo* sounds that sounded like canine amusement.

Paul, who was getting spattered by association, let go of Dabney and began pushing llamas away, his smile contained behind an expression of absolute astonishment.

The llamas finally stopped their assault as Ed and his helpers waded among them, shoving and yelling. Dabney looked down at her ruined leather outfit, her mouth slack, her hands dangling.

*You she-Elvis, you've been slimed,* Caroline thought victoriously. She glanced down and found Wolf gazing at her.

"That'll teach her to mess with our man, won't it?" she whispered.

Wolf yipped.

Caroline clamped a hand over her mouth and stopped breathing. *Had she told the llamas to spit on Dabney?* No, she hadn't tried, she hadn't even thought . . .

*Had they sensed what she wanted?*

Yes. Oh, Lord, yes. They'd felt her jealousy and reacted to it. Maybe they'd felt it all the way over in the pasture and come to her aid. This was incredible.

Stunned by the force of her feelings for Paul and what they'd unwittingly accomplished, Caroline turned quickly and headed for the house. She had to think this over.

"Hey, llama mama, watch out!" Paul yelled.

Caroline turned around and gasped. The whole herd was following her respectfully. They crowded around her.

A few reached out and touched their noses to her gently. There was no spitting. People who'd been guffawing hysterically now watched dumbfounded. She glanced over the llamas' heads and saw Paul with his hands on his hips, staring at her.

Caroline coughed, clasped her hands behind her back, and smiled at the llamas.

*You're very dear and I love you all. Now go back to the pasture.*

She called to the human audience, "They like blondes! I've seen llamas do this before!"

That explanation missed *weak* and went straight to *ludicrous*, she thought, but it was the best her rattled brain could do.

As the llamas walked calmly, unguided, back to their pasture, Caroline walked numbly, her face burning, to the house.

The last golden streaks of sunset slanted through the open kitchen window and created yellow auras around the four cats who sat on the window ledge telling Caroline what they'd like for dinner.

"How about the tuna and cheese combination?" she asked, holding up a can with one hand and an opener with the other. She watched their faces and listened to an assortment of cat talk.

"Okay, Tabby and Orange, you'd rather eat rocks than this. I get the message, smart butts. I'll give the tuna-cheese delight to Blackie and White Kitty."

She thought wryly that if Paul ever had children, he'd better let his wife name them. That musing produced a wistful envy inside her, and she quickly distracted herself.

Caroline held another can in front of Tabby and Orange. "How about liver?"

Their eyes gleamed. *Mouse!*

Which she interpreted as *We like that.*

"Marvelous," Caroline said dryly, and began opening the can.

"Tell me, *chère*, would they like spoons and napkins?"

Caroline turned around and saw Paul standing in the doorway, one long leg out at an angle, his hands on his hips, a thoughtful smile softening his blunt-featured face as he watched her and the cats.

Oh, that knowing smile of his was bad, very bad. At this rate he was going to figure out everything about her, including her special talent with animals and the fact that her heart raced every time she looked at him.

"Animals respond automatically to the sound of a soothing human voice," she answered. "And cats especially like female voices."

"What do llamas like?"

"I don't know." She looked at him innocently. "That was a fascinating incident today." She busied herself with the cat food, glancing at him as she did. "I believe this is the first time I've seen you clean and fully dressed, doc."

"Look." He pointed to his comfortable brown loafers.

"Feet. I'd recognize them anywhere."

"Not that. Look. No socks." His voice was droll. "See? I can be fashionable too, yes?"

She chuckled. "Indeed."

Caroline's arms tingled with pleasant goose bumps as he crossed the room and sat on the kitchen table near her. She felt his gaze burning into her back.

"Thanks for feeding my cats," he offered.

"No problem. I like cats with practical names. Are you ready to go?"

He clapped his hands together. "*Mais oui!* Ready for *le bon temps!* Good times!"

Caroline glanced at him distractedly. Every woman in the state must be dying to share *le bon temps* with Dr. Blue, pure masculinity in a casual package.

He wore a long-sleeved white pullover of heavy cotton that resembled a football jersey. It was decorated with a broad band of blue around the chest and shoulders, and he'd tucked the jersey into faded jeans.

His flowing black hair and deep tan looked even more exotic next to the white pullover, his eyes more blue because of the complementing band of color across his chest, his shoulders more muscular where the color emphasized them. Breathing in shallow puffs, Caroline looked down at the can she had opened. "Ooops. Wrong one. Chicken."

White Kitty yowled in dismay.

Paul laughed. "Sounds like she's mad."

She is, Caroline told him silently. She hates chicken.

"Hey, Caro, you gotta change clothes. All those scarves and shawls and things—people will think you got no closet."

"Caro? *Caro?* Pick a better nickname, please. That sounds like a syrup. Now, what's this about me wearing too many clothes?"

"You'll get hot."

The skirt and blouse combination with layers of accessories was straight from a Neiman-Marcus display. Annoyed, she pointed to her heart. "I'm cold-natured."

"Once you eat some spicy Cajun food you're gonna strip like a table dancer at a nudie bar. The dance of the overpriced scarves. Besides, people will think you're a snob if you dress like that."

"I am a snob, and proud of it."

"Nah, not really. Go change."

Huffing, she crossed the kitchen to her bedroom door. When she jerked the door open, a blast of cool air rolled out. Just before she shut the door behind her she whirled around and gleefully thumbed her nose at him.

"Thanks for the A.C. and the fashion advice."

He blew her a kiss.


His classic black Corvette convertible made a perfect picture against the cathedral-like avenue of oak trees beyond the mansion's lawn. A low fog was creeping in from the marshes, and it swirled around the car in the dusky evening light. The air was pleasantly warm and laden with the scents of earth and greenery.

An advertising genius couldn't have created a better atmosphere. If an automobile could be sexy and mysterious, the Corvette was the ultimate seducer.

Standing on the patio, Caroline braced a hand against one of the mansion's majestic columns, seeking support. The mental image of Paul behind the wheel of the Corvette sent a white-hot arc of sensation through her.

"Hey, doc, you told me you drive an old truck," she murmured over her shoulder.

"I do sometimes." Paul finished locking the front door and came to stand beside her. He looked down at her with proud, teasing eyes. "A man shouldn't reveal all his goodies at once."

"That's one terrific goodie. Which bothers you more—when men drool or women throw themselves on the hood?"

He chuckled. "You like it. *Bien.* I got it, oh, ten, twelve years ago, when I was in college. It was a mess, a real fixer-upper."

He worked so damned hard to get and keep everything he owned. He poured energy and commitment into everything he touched. How could she help but feel this surge of affection for him?

Paul leaned against a column across from hers and watched her for a moment. "You okay, *chère*?"

"Of course." It was a lie. She couldn't bear to look at him, afraid that she'd cry and ask him to hold her. The air seemed vividly sweet and enticing; the small night songs of insects came to her underscored by the faint sound of slow, moaning jazz music that tightened her belly with erotic yearnings.

Caroline dug her fingernails into her palms. It was some kind of Cajun magic Blue had conjured up to ruin her defenses.

"Caroline?" Paul said worriedly.

Ed Thompson had a collection of New Orleans jazz albums, she recalled, trying desperately to be sensible. The music must be coming from his cabin.

"I'm . . . just tired, that's all."

Caroline clutched her chest as if she couldn't breathe. She had to get away from Blue and this place.

"You okay?" he asked again, and stepped toward her.

She straightened swiftly and glared at him. "I'm fine, Dr. Dolittle. Stop hovering."

He halted, studying her and frowning. With a sudden overwhelming ache she knew what was happening to her; she was homesick for a home she'd never known and dying to fall in love with this man.

*Stop it!*

"What's goin' on in that she-devil mind of yours?" he teased, but his eyes were serious.

Caroline shoved one hand into the pocket of the black slacks she wore with an off-the-shoulder black sweater, black flats, and an array of delicate gold jewelry. With her other hand she flipped a smooth cascade of reddish-blond hair off each shoulder. She gave Paul a disgusted look.

"You know, doc, Dabney would look great in that car. Have you shown it to her?"

"Nooo," he said in a low, wary tone.

"You ought to. If anything could make a woman forget llama spit and think about sex, your macho machine would do it."

"I'm sort of like a llama. I prefer blondes."

"You're a man. You prefer to have a friendly, willing woman." It made her a little sick to realize how easily the obnoxious act came to her.

She gazed at him in surprise when he heaved a sigh of relief. "I see," he said succinctly, as if he'd just figured out something new about her. Then he rolled his eyes, shook his head, and smiled as if she were a wayward child.

"Come on, llama mama. And cut the crap." He ambled down the walkway toward the Corvette and waved one hand in a nonchalant "follow-me" gesture.

He hadn't bought the nasty routine at all. He could see right through her and he knew she was running scared.

Her face burning with embarrassment, Caroline followed him.

It was a typical Friday night, and half the parish seemed to be at Beaujean's, a dance hall and restaurant on the outskirts of a hamlet some Cajun with a sense of humor had named Breaux LaMonde. Paul always thought that the name made Breaux LaMonde sound bigger and fancier than it was.

There was nothing fancy about Beaujean's long, low building with its neon alligator sign, but there didn't need to be. The appeal was intangible, but like most things Cajun, it would charm anyone who gave it a chance.

Paul guided a rather subdued Caroline inside a noisy dining room where the decor featured paneled walls dotted with beer signs and practical wooden chairs and tables covered with plain white cloths.

Waitresses swayed among the tables, balancing plates of steaming seafood and pitchers of beer. In one corner a four-man band was testing sound equipment.

One band member raised a mug and yelled, "Ah do ba-lieve it's Monsieur Belue, the movie star! How you doin', *cher*?"

"*Comme-ci, comme-ça,*" he answered, grinning.

Out of the corner of her mouth Caroline said to him, "Is that good?"

"Fair to middlin'."

The crowd included young and old, families and couples, all neatly dressed, which gave the raucous atmosphere a wholesome touch despite the copious amounts of beer. A mural on one wall depicted a bayou surrounded by cypress trees. On the dock of a levee an old man sat fishing.

Painted across the bottom of the mural in big, flowing script were the words *Laissez le bon temps rouler!*

Caroline pointed to the words. "Shop at Fred's fish market?"

Paul laughed, "Let the good times roll. You'll hear that a lot around here."

He watched as Caroline's sleek black outfit drew stares from everyone. The off-the-shoulder sweater was modest by most standards, but it exposed a tantalizing portion of her upper chest and molded itself to pretty breasts no man could resist studying. She had long, slender legs, and the black slacks were a perfect way to show them off.

By the time she slid into the chair Paul held out, her face had the shuttered look he was getting to know so well. "They're staring at me," she whispered. She sat very straight and casually let a swathe of red-gold hair cover her scar.

He sat down across from her and leaned forward with a conspiratorial wink. "They think you're a movie star."

"Hah." She glanced around. "It's very, ummm, down-home. Everyone looks like they just came from a PTA meeting." She paused, frowning. "They look friendly, but I wish most of them weren't speaking French."

He took her hand. It was icy. "Relax, Caroline. How about some beer?"

"*Oui.*" She nodded almost desperately. "Oh, *oui.*"

Two beers later she had her elbows on the table and her hair shoved behind her ears. Paul coaxed her to tell stories about her work with famous animal actors and blessed his intuition when eagerness came into her eyes. He loved listening to her voice and watching her face.

Each time she laughed or smiled he caught his breath a little. A world of kindness lay deep inside her, and it showed as she talked about her work with animals.

When dinner came she stared down at it, and her humor faded. "What did you order for me? Where's the person who's supposed to help me eat it? Why are those crawfish so red? Are they embarrassed? They ought to be, because this is an outrageous amount of food."

"*Dieu!*" he exclaimed, laughing. "Look, it's a combination." He pointed to different specialties. "Fried 'gator, fried catfish, boiled crawdads, stuffed crab, jambalaya, and a cup of gumbo. Be careful. It's all spicy."

She took a bite of crab and her eyes watered. He handed her a glass of beer; she swallowed a gulp of it and sighed. "I like it."

"*Bien!* Can you finish it?"

"Sure. The first bite nuked my taste buds. They're numb."

By the time they finished dinner, the band cranked up its first song, a rousing tune that got many of the diners on their feet. The singer belted the French lyrics out in a nasal yodel.

"Sounds as if he's hollering for help," Caroline observed drolly, but her fingertips were keeping time on the table.

"It's 'La Porte en Arrière.' It's very popular—sort of a Cajun national anthem."

"*Bien!*" she said loudly.

He looked at her with amusement. She gave him a crooked smile. "I've had too much beer. I don't usually drink."

"Say something else in French."

She thought for a moment, then drew herself up proudly and pointed toward the mural. "*Latex la bon tom Rolaids.*"

Paul laughed until his stomach hurt. When he finally managed to stop he noticed that her smile had faded into a pensive look.

"I don't drink much because my mother's drinking was responsible for this." She gestured toward her scar.

He grimaced. "Oh, no, *chère,* this isn't a night for brooding, no. Forget about your mother. Come on."

Before her mood could turn darker, he led her to the dance floor. The music was a twangy mixture of accordion, guitar, fiddle, and drums with a fast rhythm.

"Can you two-step, *chère*?"

"Certainly!"

"Ow. I said two-step, not toe-step."

"Sorry. Keep your feet out of my way."

"My feet are supposed to lead, you she-devil. I'm the boy, you're the girl, and—"

"Okay, okay, quit beating your chest and hold me against it. I'll do whatever you do."

That offer was too good to tamper with, so he pulled her to him and suffered her stomping gladly. Several songs later she had mastered both the two-step and the waltz, and then she looked up at him with excited, half-shut eyes as if she were experiencing something new and much more delicious than dancing.

"I absolutely love this."

Paul nearly groaned. "I can't concentrate if you look at me that way," he warned in a solemn voice.

"What way?"

"What way? she says. Don't the men in Beverly Hills tell you how sexy you look when you dance?"

"Sure. All the time."

"Lots of men, yes?"

Her guarded look came back. "Several."

"Anyone special?"

"They're all special, each in his own way."

"Tell me about them."

She laughed, sounding a little awkward. "They're all handsome and wealthy."

"You're not talking, right?"

"Right."

Paul wondered if she had someone important in California, or at least someone she cared about. Nah. Why would the brutally honest Caroline be evasive when he asked her about it?

"So what are they doing while you're in Louisiana?"

She smiled wickedly. "Crying."

"Why? Afraid you'll come back?"

"Oooh, mean!"

She slapped his cheek playfully; he turned his head and caught her thumb between his teeth, then sucked it for a second before he turned loose. Her lashes flickered and a languorous pink mist crept over her face.

Paul nearly groaned. He looked away from the tempting sight and wished for several things—first, that they were in his bedroom; second, that she weren't tipsy, because he wouldn't want her to regret anything after she sobered up; and third, that he could think of an excuse to avoid the slow dance the band would probably play next.

Holding her closer would be torture. Wanting her was a special hell because he knew that she wanted him, too, but not the people or the place that he represented. He was certain that he could win her over and bring to light all the tenderness she tried to hide, but he needed more time.

"I have to go play the accordion," he murmured as the band finished its song.

The band leader announced in a low, wicked tone, "We gonna do one of them snugglin' songs next."

"You have to play the accordion now?" she asked gruffly.

Her yearning tone only added to his distress. "Now," he told her firmly, as if world peace depended on it.

Paul took her hand and they went to the band's corner. He motioned to the man who'd greeted him earlier. "Hey, Felix, I'm ready to take over."

"Huh?" Felix looked at him blankly.

Paul glared at him. "Caroline, meet Felix Chavis. Felix, Caroline Fitzsimmons. Felix, ma ladyfriend is waitin' to hear me play the accordion."

"Oh!"

Felix had finally caught on, thankfully. With a great sigh of relief Paul found Caroline a chair near the band, grabbed the accordion from Felix, and held it low in front of his body. The accordion made a great screen for a man's dignity, he thought.

He played several songs with the band, and her incredulous smile told him that she was caught up in the music and impressed by his skill. The music was charged with emotion; it wailed, coaxed, wept, and laughed heartily, conveying both the sadness and the joy of Cajun history.

Paul's gaze kept meeting Caroline's; each time the atmosphere between them pulsed with excitement. When the band took a break, he walked to her slowly, never giving her a moment's respite.

Breathing between parted lips, her face flushed sexily, she stood up and motioned for him to bend his head. Her breath was warm on his cheek, and the scent of her skin and hair was a potent aphrodisiac. He'd bet money that her perfume had one of those provocative names.

She whispered, "You're great with that thing."

He gave her a slow, intimate look. "I'll be glad to play anytime you want."

She laughed shakily. "You make the music come alive."

"The look on your face gives me inspiration, *chère*. I could make music all night for you."

"You play much better with clothes on, but it's not as interesting to watch."

They grinned like old friends, and he realized that he was having the time of his life. With a certainty that amazed him, Paul knew that he and this woman could turn the world inside out for each other.

•  •  •

The next morning he got up early, glad that it was Saturday and there was no movie work scheduled. He pulled a pair of cutoffs on and hurried down the long, creaking staircase, planning to surprise Caroline with a big breakfast.

The last time he'd seen her she'd had her shoes in one hand and a daffy smile on her face. She'd been leaning against her bedroom door and blowing him sleepy good-night kisses.

This morning Wolf—who usually slept in Paul's bedroom—met him at the bottom of the stairs, his ears and tail drooping. Paul gave him a shrewd look, cursed loudly, and ran to the kitchen.

On the far side, the door to the small bedroom stood open.

While his breath stalled in his throat, Paul walked into the room. The air conditioner was turned off. The bed was neatly made. Her things were gone. She was gone.

He'd never felt more alone.

# *Five*

Paul cuddled the miniature zebra's head in one hand and carefully put drops in her infected eye with the other. She was just a baby, barely four months old, and no taller than his knees. Her dam stood nearby in the small paddock, watching intently.

"There, *ma petite fille*, you'll be fine."

The foal drew a lungful of fragrant morning air, then exhaled it in a playful snort. Paul tucked the bottle of antibiotic drops into a pocket of his work shirt and stroked her ears as he straightened wearily, his body stiff from two nights of camping out on a marsh island.

"Blue, come look at something. I don't know what to make of this. The ferrets have turned into little zombies."

Paul turned and found Ed frowning by the pen's gate.

"I know how they feel."

Paul left the pen and walked with him through two barns, crossed an open area in the compound, and stopped at the ferrets' habitat. Despite his fatigue and bad mood, he stared at the small animals with fascination.

All two dozen of them sat upright by the wire fence, their tiny paws tucked against their chests, their manner expectant but not alarmed, their sharp, dark eyes trained on some invisible something beyond the staff buildings.

Ed scratched his head and sighed. "Cat came out of the woods a minute ago. He's lying by his moat. Waiting. Just like the ferrets. The llamas are all lined up by the pasture fence, like some sort of reception line at a party."

"Think we're about to have an earthquake or something?"

"No. But what?"

Paul scanned a peaceful panorama of marsh and woodland, then raised his gaze to a magnificent blue sky. "Couldn't be the weather." He frowned. "Seen Wolf lately?"

"No."

"If there's a good reason for everything to be upset, he'll be that way too."

Ed shrugged, his dark eyes intrigued. "They don't look upset. They look excited."

"I'll find Wolf." Paul walked quickly toward the house. He climbed a small rise, passed along a path bordered by a wooden fence covered in honeysuckle vines, and strode under the giant oaks that surrounded the main grounds.

He spotted Wolf in the grass at the edge of the driveway, his posture quiet and sphinxlike as he gazed down the shadowy corridor of oaks that canopied the road. Paul watched him curiously. What in the world was going on here?

"Wolf. *Venez! Marchons!*"

Wolf stood at the orders, looked over his shoulder at Paul, wagged his magnificent plumed tail tentatively, then looked back down the road. Paul went to him and knelt, running a hand over Wolf's thick silver ruff.

"What are you expecting, *ami*?"

Paul glanced up and saw a long black limousine pull

into sight at the distant curve in the drive. He drew a sharp breath. It was only eight A.M., but this must be Caroline returning from the weekend.

He cursed the bittersweet anticipation that tugged at him. Anger overwhelmed it as he dug his palms into the faded denim of his jeans.

She'd gone to California to take care of the need he'd created in her. She'd taken the passion he'd cherished and given it to some other man—why else would she sneak away without offering him the honor of an explanation or a good-bye?

She hadn't had the honesty or the courage to make love with him. He'd thought that he understood her, but he was wrong. He'd thought that deep down they shared the same need for friendship and tenderness as well as sex. He was wrong.

There was a wide streak of tolerance in him; he tried to look inside people and animals, then understand their motivations without passing judgment. He got angry easily, and he forgave easily too. But this he couldn't forgive.

"No more foolishness for me, *chère*," he said fiercely. "I've learned my lesson."

He certainly wasn't going to stand here like a wistful kid, waiting to greet her. He stood, feeling miserable and furious, swung about on one heel, and walked back toward the wild animal compound.

All four of his cats bolted out of the honeysuckle. Two of them dived between his work boots, nearly tripping him. They headed for the driveway at top speed.

Paul came to an astonished halt. Caroline's arrival was responsible for the animals' strange behavior, he realized.

No, that was ridiculous. It went beyond rational explanation. He'd worked with animals all his life and he'd never seen anything like this before.

Paul rammed his hands through his hair. He'd never seen anyone like Caroline Fitzsimmons before either.

Okay. Think. She used some subtle training technique to make animals respond to her this way.

*Sure, man. And that makes them sense that she's arriving before they see her.*

No, that was a damned impossibility. Then what? Some psychic connection? Paul grimaced with disgust at that notion. In New Orleans there were modern-day voodoo witches who said they could control animals and people through their magic. He found voodoo at least as reasonable as psychic mumbo-jumbo.

Paul shook his head, slapped the air violently with one hand, and walked on. Bewitched, then. She'd bewitched his animals, but she'd sure as hell lost her chance to bewitch him.

*Master sad. Hurt. Miss you.*

Caroline inhaled raggedly and cupped Wolf's head in her hands. She'd barely had time to swing her feet out of the limo before he shoved past the driver and plopped his large gray head on her knees.

*When Master with you—good. You stay!*

*I had to go away and think. Where is he, Wolf?*

Wolf took her hand in his mouth and tugged gently. *Follow.*

Caroline managed to tell the driver where to leave her suitcases before Wolf dragged her away from the limo. He was so impatient that she almost toppled over on the stiletto heels of her scarlet shoes, and had to withdraw her hand from his grip.

The rest of her was the same fiery shade of red as the shoes—her voluminous silk jacket with padded shoulders that a defensive tackle would envy, the cowl-neck blouse underneath, and the slinky, tapering pants with their scarlet buttons at the ankles.

She'd wound her hair up in a knot and adorned it with a scarlet and gold comb. Even the rims of her sunglasses blazed with the warning red color.

It was the kind of outrageous outfit women called dramatic and men called embarrassing; it would surely help in her campaign to keep distance between herself and Paul.

Wait a minute. Weren't bulls enraged by bright reds? Caroline shook the anxious thought away and followed Wolf down a path bordered by honeysuckle bushes taller than her head.

She and Wolf came in sight of the movie crew, who were eating breakfast at long tables on the lawn in front of the caterer's trailer. People stopped what they were doing, turned around in their chairs, and stared unabashedly at her.

Caroline waved at Frank, who stood up with his mouth ajar and pointed behind her. She glanced back.

She was being trailed by four cats, a small squadron of white ducks from the plantation's pond, and a squirrel.

Caroline winced. Blue's animals were truly dear, but this was getting out of control. "They like the color," she called stoically, pointed to her outfit, and trudged on.

Now her face matched her clothes.

Wolf led her to Paul's veterinary hospital, a small white stucco building nestled beside a barn. Wolf settled on its concrete stoop. Caroline turned toward the rest of her menagerie.

*Sweet babies. Now go about your business before a freak show asks me to audition.* They scattered politely.

Caroline took a deep breath, swung a plain wood door open, and stepped into an anteroom that smelled of antiseptic and medicine. A couple of male college students sat at battered desks amid stacks of books.

"We're trying to figure out why the panther won't mate," one of them explained. "We don't have a female panther of his species, but we've got a female cougar from Texas. At least we could get genetically similar cross-bred kittens, but he won't have anything to do with her."

"Sounds like a problem for Dr. Ruth."

The boys grinned.

Caroline pointed toward a closed office door. "Blue's?"

"Yes."

She went over and knocked, wishing her heart weren't drumming in her chest.

"Yeah," she heard him say. His deep, slightly accented tone sent shivers down her spine and made her breath pull short. Caroline squared her shoulders, straightened her sunglasses, and invaded Blue's small office with haughty grandeur.

He sat at an old wood desk cluttered with files and letters. The floor was stacked with professional journals, charts were thumbtacked to every available inch of wall space, and his bookshelves overflowed with medical texts. This was one place where the Belue penchant for spareness and simplicity had failed to take hold.

*Because he cares so much about his work*, she thought with admiration.

His head jerked up at the sight of her, his blue eyes flaring, his mouth a grim line of distaste. His long black hair was ragged, as if he'd been running his fingers through it violently. He flattened his big hands on the desktop and leaned forward, a muscle flexing in his jaw. He radiated a crackling energy that made him seem bigger, more dangerous, and more breathtaking than she'd remembered.

"This building is off limits to Hollywood people."

Caroline fought to keep from gaping at him. Her proud demeanor nearly drained away in the face of his hostility. She'd expected him to be puzzled, maybe a little angry, but not furious.

"I . . . I just came to tell you that I was back and that I'd take charge of Wolf on the set today."

"Fine. I'll let you take care of him from now on. Just stay out of my way, 'cause I'm busy, see? Good-bye. I have work to do."

She raised her brows at him and shot back, "And a lovely Monday morning to you too."

Caroline pivoted on one heel and strode to the door. His voice assaulted her with low, controlled anger.

"Was he worth the long trip home? Did he take care of the itch I gave you, yes?"

Shock poured through her. Of course he'd think that she'd returned to California for the weekend to see one of the man friends she'd mentioned.

The ridiculous pads in her jacket shoulders disguised the sudden slumping of her back. This was for the best, she told herself. The perfect way to keep Paul from pursuing her anymore.

"He was terrific," she answered softly, and slammed the door behind her as she left the room.


It was a good thing Paul's animals adored her, because they were her only company.

She barely saw him over the next two weeks. Caroline found herself keeping a quiet vigil on the movie set. When they filmed in the marshes bordering the barns she strained her eyes to glimpse Paul as he walked from one to the other.

When they filmed in the mansion she kept a watch on the doors, hoping that he'd have some reason to come in during the day. He never did.

Rain poured down one night. Caroline got out of bed and opened her window so that she could inhale the wet, fresh darkness. She was startled when she heard a phone ring upstairs, followed by hurried sounds.

She identified Paul's heavy footsteps plus the clicking cadence of Wolf's feet as Wolf followed him; the two rhythms descended the long front staircase quickly and ran out the front doors.

There must be an emergency; she recalled hearing Ed say that an elderly gazelle had developed pneumonia.

Caroline considered the consequences for a moment, then threw some clothes on and ran after Paul. There was too much at stake to let his anger or her defensiveness intrude.

She headed for the veterinary building, where lights blazed with watery luminescence in the heavy rain. Soaked and shivering, Caroline burst into the anteroom. Wolf, dripping water, got up from his place on a muddy rug and came to her, his eyes solemn.

*Master needs you.*

*I'll help him.*

One of the students, a veterinary intern she'd met before, came through double doors at the back of the building's central hallway. Her eyes were swollen from crying.

She stopped at the sight of Caroline and wiped them with quick, embarrassed motions. "Yes?"

"I came to see the gazelle."

The young woman sighed raggedly. "Dr. Blue's with her in the back. She's dying."

Caroline ran past her. The woman gasped and grabbed for her arm. "You can't." But Caroline was already shoving the doors open by then. She walked swiftly through the large-animal quadrant of the hospital, a snug, brightly lit place of large stalls and concrete floors.

Her heart racing with dread, Caroline stopped by an open stall door and stared at an array of sophisticated equipment that surrounded a small, fragile creature that must have been designed as a fairy's steed.

It lay on its side on a blanket, tubes crisscrossing its fawn-color body. Its eyes were closed and it breathed with a labored, rattling sound.

Paul, his hair and work denims slicked to his wet body, sat beside the gazelle. He had a stethoscope pressed to its chest, and his head was bowed in an

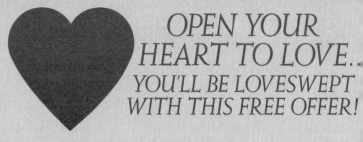

# FREE – LIGHTED MAKEUP CASE!
# FREE – 6 LOVESWEPT NOVELS!

- NO OBLIGATION
- NO PURCHASE NECESSARY

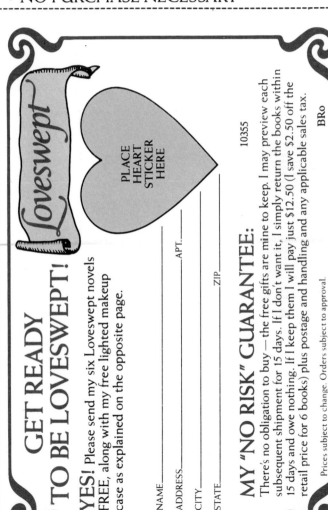

## GET READY TO BE LOVESWEPT!

**YES!** Please send my six Loveswept novels FREE, along with my free lighted makeup case as explained on the opposite page.

*Loveswept*

PLACE
HEART
STICKER
HERE

NAME _____

ADDRESS _____ APT. ____

CITY _____

STATE _____ ZIP _____

10355

## MY "NO RISK" GUARANTEE:

There's no obligation to buy — the free gifts are mine to keep. I may preview each subsequent shipment for 15 days. If I don't want it, I simply return the books within 15 days and owe nothing. If I keep them I will pay just $12.50 (I save $2.50 off the retail price for 6 books) plus postage and handling and any applicable sales tax.

BRo

Prices subject to change. Orders subject to approval.

# REMEMBER!

- The free books and gift are mine to keep!
- There is no obligation!
- I may preview each shipment for 15 days!
- I can cancel anytime!

attitude that conveyed both concentration and weary defeat.

Caroline crept into the stall and knelt by the gazelle. Paul's head snapped up, and he looked at her in astonishment, his eyes trailing down her soaked body.

As he removed the stethoscope Caroline gazed at him stoically, knowing that her hair was slicked back so that her scar must look particularly ugly against the side of her face and that her choice of clothes was not the most practical—tangerine trousers and an oversize purple shirt covered in sequins and gilded butterfly appliqués.

His expression became hard, a retaining wall that kept his emotions in check, by the time his gaze rose to her face. He held her neutral green-gold eyes for a long moment, his blue ones intense and searching. Slowly he nodded toward the gazelle.

"You can do something that will help her, yes?" he asked hoarsely, and the resistance drained out of him.

Caroline's throat burned with unshed tears. He cared so much for his animals that he would discard his pride gladly if she could save the gazelle's life.

"I'm not a healer," she said truthfully.

"She's too far gone for that, even if you were. You create comfort and trust somehow. Do that for her. Let her die in peace, at least."

"All right." Caroline lay down by the gazelle and snuggled an arm around her neck. The touch ignited knowledge swiftly and sadly; Paul was right, it was too late. It was the gazelle's time; she was old and unhappy, and she wanted to die. But she was afraid to let go.

*Sleep. It's safe. You're not alone.*

The gazelle's breathing became less tortured. Tears in her eyes, Caroline looked up to find Paul's frowning, deciphering gaze on her. He didn't want to like her or believe in her, she thought sadly, and the realization was almost unbearable.

"Go back to the house. I'll do better here alone," she told him crisply. "I'm quite cynical about death and dying. I don't need you to stare at me and wonder what it is I do that makes animals feel better. I just . . . I just understand how to give affection to animals. Other than children, they're the only things on God's green earth that are worth the effort."

Something tragic crept into his gaze, and he looked sad rather than forbidding. "Aw, *chère,* you know so little about the world."

He rose to his feet. She blinked back tears and a traitorous desire to ask him to stay. He looked down at her grimly. "Anna will be here all night to check on things. Thank you for coming to help. You're not so heartless as you'd like to think, no."

He left the stall quickly, as if that were the only way he could make himself go, and Caroline blessed the fact that the first tear didn't slide down her cheek until after he departed.

What a woman. What a bewildering, frustrating, heart-breaking woman, Paul thought as he sat in a rocking chair by his bedroom window, staring out at the black night and the rain. He hadn't changed clothes; he didn't attempt to sleep.

His thoughts were bonded to the odd scene he'd left in the hospital; Caroline as beautiful and sleek as any high-fashion model, even soaked with Louisiana rain, even with the scar that caused her so much torment; Caroline lying there in the coarse confines of a concrete stall hugging a gazelle as if it were her child.

He didn't understand her; he'd never understand her, probably. He didn't understand his dangerous need for her and the tenderness she created inside him with her perplexing vulnerability. No. *No.*

He'd loved before, but never enough to lose his ability

to reason. This had to be conquered, this foolish impulse to break down her defenses at all costs. She couldn't be won; she wasn't meant to be tied to one man or stay in Louisiana among her memories.

Not long before dawn the rain slacked to a warm drizzle. Feeling ancient, nothing resolved, Paul got up and walked back to the hospital. Anna sat at the desk in the anteroom.

She shook her head at him wretchedly. "It's almost over. I checked ten minutes ago."

His eyes grainy, Paul quietly opened the doors to the large-animal section. Someone had dimmed all the lights except the one over the gazelle's stall. Wolf lay just outside its open door, his head on his paws.

The tip of his tail fluttered in greeting, but he seemed weighted down by the impending presence of death.

Paul walked softly to the door and stopped, his throat twisting.

Caroline knelt beside the gazelle, her fingers brushing tenderly over the tiny, fine-boned head. Anna had removed all the tubes.

"You're free now," Paul heard Caroline whisper in a gentle voice. "There. Go home. I feel it, yes. Go home. No more pain, no more fear. Yes, you're safe. That's right, you're not old and sick anymore. Go on, go on. Yes, I see the light, I see it."

What did she see? What did all this mean? Paul shook his head. It was just the way she talked to animals, commiserating with them as if she knew what they felt. It was part of her technique.

Caroline rested her forehead against the gazelle's neck. Her other hand tightened on the animal's shoulder, then stroked tenderly.

"Good-bye," she murmured. "It's wonderful. I *understand*. You're not alone anymore. Good-bye, sweetheart, good-bye."

After a long, tortured moment, Paul whispered, "None of us has to be alone, unless we want it that way."

Caroline looked up slowly, her eyes limpid with sorrow but also glowing with awe. It was the most amazing sight, and he stared at her as if he'd just glimpsed heaven. What had she seen?

"Some creatures are meant to live and die alone," she said, and the light faded from her eyes.

He sighed in disagreement, knelt beside the gazelle, and checked the silent artery in her neck. He caressed the gazelle's head. "Others will be born to take your place," he promised gruffly. "We won't let your kind disappear."

Caroline made a crying sound. "I wish I were a healer."

"Shhh. You were her friend. You kept her from being afraid tonight." He held his hand out. "Enough. You need to rest. *Allez.*"

She took his hand and wobbled upright, exhausted from the hours she'd spent by the gazelle. Paul led her from the stall, but she stopped so that she could look back one more time.

"I see that you're very cynical about these things, just the way you told me you were," he said gently.

She ducked her head in chagrin and walked ahead of him, her movements hampered by fatigue and stiffness. When she stumbled leaving the building, Paul caught her by one elbow.

Before she could protest he swung her up in his arms. Shocked, she clasped the front of his shirt desperately and held on. "This isn't necessary, doc."

"I owe you one," he said simply. "Relax."

The comfort in his voice pushed a button inside her; she rested her dried, matted hair against his shoulder and was asleep by the time he reached the house. Her childlike response flooded his chest with tenderness, but again a perturbing question ate at him—would he ever understand this complicated woman?

Once inside the house Paul hesitated at the base of the staircase. Then, his decision made, he carried her up to his room, put her on his bed, and sat down beside her.

"What?" she asked groggily as soon as her body settled on the unaccustomed luxury of his big, comfortable mattress.

"Sleep, *chère*, sleep. You can go back to your own bed tomorrow. I'll sleep there tonight." He ran his fingertips over her face, studying her in the darkness, coaxing her to be still.

A languid shudder ran through her. "The things you do with your touch"—she said the words vaguely, but with a thread of worry—"cause trouble."

"For both of us," he agreed, and quickly sat back. Paul grasped her feet and removed her wet jogging shoes. Then he clamped a hand on her knee and squeezed for attention. "Get undressed, *chère*. Don't lay here and catch cold."

"Okay." She rolled over on one side, curled her hands under her chin, and went back to sleep.

"Caroline," Paul whispered in exasperation. When there was no answer, he reached around her and unfastened her fashionably baggy trousers.

She stirred a little when he anchored both big hands in the floppy material around her ankles. He knelt by her feet and gracefully whipped the trousers down her legs. Gasping, she flopped over on her back and tried to jerk her feet away from him.

"Doc? Doc Belue! Blue! Paul!"

"That about covers it, yes," he quipped as he lifted one foot and pulled the trousers off, then did the other. "Or *uncovers* it. *Dieu!*"

She crossed her legs and clasped her hands over herself. "I didn't have time for panties."

Paul stared down at the spot her hands covered, then at the pale, luscious hips unmarred by evidence of lingerie. He got up and slung a blanket over her, then stood beside the bed frozen with control, his fists clenched.

"I'm sorry," she whispered.

"I'm not mad at you. I'm just trying to remember all the reasons why I shouldn't want you."

"Then I'm not sorry," she murmured, her voice strained. "There's nothing I'd like better than to be held in your arms. Just to be held . . . to share what we feel about the gazelle. That's all I ask."

She sat up, her lower body covered by the blanket and her upper body still covered by her shirt. Paul almost groaned when she held out her arms to him. "I swear," she said tearfully. "I don't want to seduce you, because I know you'd resent me for it later. Can't we just be friends for a minute?"

He was tortured by the desire to offer comfort of many kinds. Lost in this vulnerable moment, he could make love to her without thinking; it would be so easy to finish undressing her and give her the tender passion she seemed to need, at least for the moment.

Paul shut his eyes and told her fiercely, "I don't want to start something that someone else would get to finish. After you go back to California I don't want to sit around here wishing that I could kill whoever you make love to."

She cried out with a tormented sound that surprised him. He looked at her as she slid from his bed, grabbing for her pants.

"Don't leave," he amended as she wrapped them around herself like a skirt. "Dammit, Caroline, I didn't mean—"

"It's all right," she said in a choked voice. "I wasn't thinking straight. It'll be better if I go to my own room."

He grabbed her shoulder and looked down at her grimly. "If you wanted the same things I do, I'd put my arms around you and never let you go."

She shivered under his touch. "What things do you want?"

"I'm a one-woman man and I want a one-man woman."

"A one-man woman who'd be content to stay here at Grande Rivage."

"Right."

"Sorry," she said, her voice breaking. "I can't do it."

He cupped her chin in one hand. "What? Be a one-man woman or live here in Louisiana?"

"Which is most important to you?"

"Both," he said immediately.

"No options, eh?" she asked wearily, then took a ragged breath. "Okay. I'll make this easy for us. I can't do either."

He let go of her and stepped back, his posture rigid. "And I can't play the field the way you do. I wish I could be modern and say 'What the hell? Who cares?' But I can't. I want commitment. I've never gone into a relationship where I didn't hope that it'd lead to marriage."

"Then why aren't you married?"

"There's someone special out there, and I've been waiting to find her."

"You're very old-fashioned. Good luck."

"Don't you ever feel that way, Caroline? That there's someone worth waiting for?"

She shifted from one foot to the other and rammed her free hand through her hair. "I . . . damn. It's late. What's the point in this discussion?"

Before he could answer she gave him a kiss on the cheek and said raggedly, "I admire old-fashioned attitudes."

Then she turned and ran from his room.


When Frank trucked everyone deep into the swamp for four hellish days and three bug-bombed nights, she grew so desperate to see Paul and hear his voice that one afternoon Wolf began whining in shared anguish.

*We go home to Master.*

*Not yet, Wolf. Master would be angry.*

*Bad you? Bad Wolf?*

*Yes. He'd think we were both bad.*

Wolf slept under her cot that night, and she hung one arm over the side so that her fingers could tangle in his ruff. Caroline dreamed wistful dreams about seeing Paul again.

When she woke up the next morning, Wolf was gone.

After she calmed down Frank and the director, she took a truck and made the long drive back to the plantation along muddy swamp roads. Caroline parked by one of the barns and climbed out gratefully. The muggy air had turned her neatly creased hiking shorts and crisp T-shirt into something resembling Paul's accordion.

She walked up behind Paul as he stood by the panther's fence, watching Cat stare at a tawny female cougar. Wolf lay at Paul's feet, facing her direction. His eyes became sly slits and he seemed to smile.

*Master wants to see you.*

Caroline couldn't concentrate on rebuking him because she was too intent on studying Paul from head to toe. He stood with his long legs braced and his arms crossed over his chest. His jeans and shirt were sweat-stained; his laced boots were covered in mud.

Caroline sighed at the way sorrow mingled with reckless excitement inside her chest. She knew now just how far gone she was. She wanted this sweaty, dirty, troublesome man with a terrifying certainty.

The cougar rolled over on her back and waved her front paws at Cat playfully.

Cat hissed at her.

"Dye her coat black," Caroline offered simply. "He'll mate with her if she doesn't look so alien to him."

Paul turned quickly, surprised. For a moment he held her eyes with a charged gaze full of potential, and she believed that he was glad to see her. Then he seemed to remember that she was as alien to him as the cougar to Cat.

"You're dressed normally for once," he observed, nodding curtly at her shorts and top.

"I can be as ordinary as the rest of the world when I want to be."

He looked down at Wolf and commanded, "Go back. Now. Do what she tells you to do and behave." He dismissed Wolf with an angry gesture toward Caroline.

She almost cried at the way Wolf slunk to her, his nobility gone, absolutely humiliated by his master's unexpected harshness. She felt as if she'd been dismissed the same way.

"Dye the cougar black," Caroline repeated, her voice weary. "It'll make Cat think she's one of his kind."

"You know a lot about deceiving males, eh?"

She drew her chin up and eyed him proudly while little rivulets of pain curled around her rib cage. "I know how to make them do what's best for them."

"You mean what's best for you."

"I thought we were discussing panthers."

"No more trips home the past two weekends. Why not, *chère*?"

"That's none of your business."

His eyes hardened even more. "Best you go home next weekend. I have company coming."

"Oh? Ordinary people actually visit you here in the bog?"

"Nothing ordinary about this visitor."

"I can't go home. We're filming next Saturday."

"Then at least be polite to her—or I'll take your air conditioner away."

She arched one red-gold brow jauntily but a knot of worry grew in her stomach. "I'd never turn my wicked California tongue loose on your mother."

"Not my mother, no. A good friend. A good woman. And her son."

Caroline put her hands on her hips and drawled, "Well, Sheriff, you don't have to worry none about us *bad* women. We'll keep to the saloon and leave the respectable family folk alone. Ceptin', of course, when we has to step out to buy more paint fer our faces and garters fer our tawdry thighs."

He almost smiled at her nonsense. Then he gritted his teeth and forced the humor away.

"Eat with the crew while she's here. I'll be using the kitchen, and I want privacy."

Caroline clenched her fists but said lightly, "So be it. When I want to leave the house I'll push the air conditioner out of my bedroom window and crawl through the opening. You won't have to see me at all."

"*Bien.*"

"*Beans* to you too, doc. Are you even going to introduce me to her?"

"Why should I?"

"If she bumps into me some night on the way to the john, I don't want her to think I'm a ghost. I prefer to spook people for better reasons."

"She won't bump into you. She'll be staying upstairs."

"Oh?" Caroline was surprised that she could continue bantering with him, considering the dread closing around her throat. "Then the only *bumping* will be the headboard of your bed?"

His eyes flashed a warning. "Not with her son here. Us old Southern boys have a code of honor."

She sighed grandly. "Too bad Sherman's not around to remind you whose honor won the Civil War."

"Yeah. Burned down Atlanta lately, Yank?"

"I'm from out west," she quipped.

"West, north. It's all Yankees. No difference."

She fluttered an imaginary fan before her face. "Why, suh, you fo'get my *fine* southern heritage on Mama's side of tha family."

"It is a fine one. Damned fine."

She dropped the invisible fan and the accent. "Tell it to the kid everybody called *Scary Carrie*. Tell it to the teenager who was willing to do anything to make boys forget the way her face looked."

The subtle shift in his expression from anger to compassion caught her off guard, and she had to fight to keep the tears out of her eyes. *What are you trying to do, girl? Make him start liking you again?*

He took a step toward her, looking troubled. Breathing hard, she took a step back. He gestured vaguely, as if trying to sum up some question of immense importance to him.

"Is that why . . . why you don't want just one man now? You have to keep proving that someone can love you?"

There was nothing accusing or ugly about his question. It was said with a hint of desperation.

Caroline swallowed until the lump in her throat was only a dull pain. "I do want just one man," she finally managed to say.

The look in his eyes seared her with its quiet intensity. "But the other night you said . . ."

"I do want just one man, okay? I told a fib. Us bad women do that sort of thing."

"One man—but not me, yes?"

The breath pooled in her lungs. She couldn't admit the truth, and it was beyond her ability at the moment to lie.

"I'd never live here," she said hoarsely. "So why discuss it? Hey—you said you go into a relationship hoping for marriage. Does this 'friend' qualify for consideration?"

"Yes. She's a widow. She wants to be a wife again."

"Ah. Well, don't worry about me and the future Mrs. Belue. I really don't want to get in your way. I'll even baby-sit her son if you want to take her dancing at Beaujean's. I'm good with children. Children and animals." She paused, then smiled grimly. "The rest of the world? Forget it."

Paul watched her silently, his head tilted to one side, his anger replaced by some utterly private emotion that made him look very tired. "I wish it could be different between you and me," he murmured.

"I have to get Wolf to the set," she countered, backing up desperately.

"Why did he run away?"

"He got bored with my company, I guess."

"No," Paul answered with soft emphasis. "You're bossy, nosy, and hardheaded, but you're never boring. And that's a compliment."

She smiled sincerely, her face hurting with the effort. "I look forward to meeting your friend."

With that enormous lie gnawing at her, she took Wolf and hurried away.


The possible Mrs. Belue was small, dark-haired, and plump in the beautiful way of women in Renaissance paintings. Her sweet face was dominated by enormous hazel eyes, and she looked very feminine in a ruffled pink blouse and demurely loose jeans.

But there was nothing naive or faltering about her softness, and when Paul introduced her to Frank and Dabney on Friday afternoon she shook their hands firmly and looked not the least bit awkward in the presence of Hollywood people.

Caroline watched surreptitiously from the corner of the mansion's cobweb-filled ballroom, where they were filming a scene in which Frederick, the kindly old swamp recluse, told gentle ghost stories to Toddy and Wolf.

All Wolf had to do was lie on the floor beside Frederick's armchair and look majestic, which came naturally to him, so it had been an easy morning's shoot.

All Caroline had to do was ignore the bittersweet jealousy clawing at her insides.

Paul cradled an adorable dark-haired boy in the crook of one muscular arm, and the child tugged affectionately at Paul's long hair. In short, Paul looked happy with the woman and her son. They made a cozy little family.

*Where were a few spitting llamas when she needed them?*

Caroline grimaced in self-rebuke. The Wicked Witch of the West, that's what she'd become if she didn't watch out.

She glanced quickly at Wolf and found him studying her with curious eyes. Panting under the huge hot lights of the set, he flopped on his side and sighed heavily.

*Master likes her. And her puppy.*

*I know, Wolf.*

*Go bite her. Chase her off.*

*No.*

Puzzlement. *You won't guard your mate?*

*Master is not my mate.*

He growled softly in disgust, fluffing his jowls out as he did. Frederick and the director were discussing the script. They froze, gazing at him worriedly.

"What's wrong with the furry dude?" the director demanded, eyeing Caroline from under a tangle of tiny red braids that hung over her forehead like a woodpecker's topknot.

"Repent, ye hound of hell," Frederick intoned in his *Macbeth* voice, glaring at the animal that had once used his leg for a territorial marker.

"Relax, he's just hot and bored," Caroline told them hurriedly. She knelt beside Wolf and tugged on his front paw. "We'll go for a walk while you guys rehearse."

Anything to get away from Paul and his guest.

Wolf shut his eyes, yawned, and didn't budge. She

gave another order. No response. Caroline squinted at him ruefully. *Meddling Wolf!*

"Caroline. I want you to meet someone."

The low, luxurious tones of Paul's voice made her shiver. He had walked up behind her. Dread pooling in her stomach, she straightened gracefully and smoothed her sweaty palms over the dark green jump suit she wore.

It was blousy and belted, with epaulets on the shoulders and giant pockets over each breast. Caroline had liked its military-chic look in the window of a Beverly Hills boutique; now she felt like a silly Ramboette next to the conservative little darling who stood beside Blue.

"Angie, this is Caroline Fitzsimmons, the animal trainer I told you about. Caroline, this is Angelique Doucet and Mark. They're from Baton Rouge."

Caroline traded a smile with her, then Mark. The child looked back with wide, fascinated eyes, then chortled in delight. "*Maman*, she's talking inside my head!"

Caroline bit her lip. *Whoops.* Most children weren't quite certain what was happening when she communicated, so they didn't mention it to their parents. To them it was a funny game, nothing out of the ordinary.

Angelique laughed and tweeked his nose. "You stop teasin', *petit.*"

"But she said '*Bonjour*' in my head!"

Caroline saw Paul's bewildered frown from the corner of her vision. She cleared her throat awkwardly. "What an imagination! How old is he?"

"Five," Angelique told her with a proud gleam in her eye.

"She already asked me how old I was," Mark noted righteously, sounding like a perturbed French elf. "Inside my head." He gave Caroline a firm look.

Caroline chuckled and resisted an inclination to hyperventilate. "I did, huh?"

"And then you said—"

"Enough of this game, *'tit* mouse!" his mother warned.

*Mark, let it be our secret,* Caroline interjected quickly.

He gazed at her a second and then, with grand drama, gave her a wink. "Okay."

She sagged inwardly with relief and looked at Angelique as if nothing strange had happened. "Are you and Mark just visiting for the weekend?"

"Yes. I teach grammar school, so I have to get home by Sunday night."

"I guess Paul told you that I'm staying in a room here. I'll be glad to baby-sit Mark if you'd like."

"I might take you up on that. Paul and I have a lot of visiting to do." She looked up at him and smiled gently. "I can't wait to see the animals and walk the land again."

Caroline watched him smile back at Angelique and began to drown inside.

Angelique—like an angel. She was a grammar school teacher—wholesomeness incarnate. And Cajun. And a doting mother. And obviously unattached to a husband. Plus she seemed to like this secluded piece of heaven as much as Blue did.

"Well, I better get back to work," Caroline said cheerfully. "Wolf, let's vamoose from these hot lights while we've got the chance." She focused on Wolf as if he required all her attention. "We've got to practice your lines for the next scene. Have to put some real emoting into that *arf arf growl.*"

Wolf stood, snuffled his nose into her outstretched hand, then turned and padded across the room and out a door.

Caroline laughed. "I guess that means I'd better hop to. Nice to meet you, Angelique." She patted Mark's leg, never looked at Paul, and glided away nonchalantly.

As Paul watched her leave, frustration knotted inside him like a heavy fist. What had he expected—that she'd resent Angelique, that she'd care whether he courted another woman? *Courted.* Lord, his language was ridiculously old-fashioned. No wonder she was always looking at him as though he were quaint.

"What's the matter, *petit*?"

Angelique was speaking to Mark. She reached up and stroked his hair lovingly. Paul twisted his head to gaze at the godson he held carefully in one brawny arm. Mark's face had a look of brave sorrow, as if someone had just told him a sad story.

"It's a secret," he said solemnly.

That evening Paul and Angelique went out to dinner, taking Mark with them. Caroline wandered restlessly around the plantation grounds. She twirled a piece of moss in her hands and sat under an oak tree at the edge of the lawn, staring into the woods, Finally she ended up at the panther habitat, where Cat sprawled cozily next to his newly dyed wife, whom Paul had named Miss Clairol.

Cat flopped a leg over Miss Clairol's black shoulders and licked her black ears. Miss Clairol nuzzled him happily.

"See what a trip to the beauty parlor can do for your love life?" Caroline called.

She went back to the house and paced back and forth in the downstairs rooms, trying to picture them without tons of camera equipment and a spider's web of cables. She'd grown to like this old home with its open, gracious feel and aura of history.

Given the chance, she could turn it into a showplace—not the kind that made people think of a museum, but something comfortable and inviting, a mixture of old styles and new.

Given a chance. *Never.* Thumping her fists lightly against her temples, Caroline retreated to her small room off the kitchen and shut the door. She put on her pajamas, got into bed, and reread a favorite Agatha Christie novel. Lord, wouldn't Paul be shocked by her choice. He probably thought she preferred those glitzy sex-and-shopping books.

When she heard the sounds of Paul's return she hugged her knees to her chest and stared at the ceiling until separate sets of doors closed upstairs. Then she flung herself on her stomach and spent the next hour morosely directing a granddaddy longlegs across the old linoleum floor.

*Go left. Go right. Make a circle.*

This was more interesting than remote control for a toy car.

Caroline jumped when she heard soft footsteps upstairs. They came down to the main level and eventually crossed the kitchen floor. Someone knocked at her door. "Caroline? Are you awake?" an accented female voice asked politely.

Angelique, the earth mother. Too bad she wasn't a granddaddy longlegs.

"Yes." Caroline threw on a robe that matched her pajamas—silky black with ornamental appliqués around the neck and sleeves. She opened the door and looked down at a smiling Angelique, who wore a fuzzy blue terry-cloth robe over some sort of ruffled pink gown.

Why, it's a Cajun June Cleaver, Caroline thought, then rubbed her forehead wearily, and rebuked herself for the petty sarcasm. "Hi. Anything wrong?"

Angelique never stopped smiling. "I'm afraid so. You're after my man."

# *Six*

"You've been misinformed."

Angelique smoothed back a neat strand of wavy brunette hair. "I've known Blue too many years to be misinformed about his feelings. Come, let's have a glass of milk and talk."

"No milk. I'm not into wholesome stuff," Caroline said wryly.

"That's why you've got to leave him alone."

Caroline propped a hand on one hip. "I've changed my mind. Make it a milk double."

They faced each other at the kitchen table, the room in darkness around them, the only light a soft circle from the old tin fixture that hung above the stove.

Angelique's mouth thinned with grim recognition. "You love him," she said firmly.

The breath rattled out of Caroline's chest. "Yes."

"Let me tell you something. The man could have as many women as he wants—a different woman every night. But he's had a total of only four lovers in his lifetime. Thirty-two years. And that includes six years he spent dating me in high school and college. I know because I'm his best friend."

"He's special," Caroline whispered. "I just didn't realize how special."

*"You don't want to hurt this man."*

"No."

Angelique waved both hands exuberantly. "Then go back to your world, where everything is disposable and everyone gets bored with everyone else in a hurry, and leave Blue to the kind of woman who can make him happy. Not ecstatic, I know that. But happy, solidly, comfortably happy. I believe he's ready to settle down now, and I intend to be the one he settles with."

Caroline frowned. "There are good, caring, loyal people outside of southern Louisiana. Frank Windham, the producer you met today, is one of them. His wife is another." Caroline raised her chin, feeling defiant and yet also hopeless. This little beauty was perfect for Paul in many ways. "I happen to consider myself a third."

*"Bien.* Then do what's honorable for Blue's sake."

Caroline bristled. "Do you really think he's ready to 'settle' for a marriage based on mutual comfort and high school memories?"

"Blue's a practical man. Surely you've noticed."

"But he's also the most vital, vibrant man I've ever known. And he's waiting for someone special."

"He's lonely and he needs help running this place. He loves children and he wants to start a family before he gets much older." Angelique slugged down her milk as if it were a fortifying shot of brandy. "Those considerations are more important than grand passion, and he knows it."

Grasping the edge of the table with a fierceness that made her fingers hurt, Caroline asked, "So why are you worried about me? I'm no competition for you in the race for domestic bliss."

"That's right. All you can do is take him to bed, confuse him, hurt him."

"You don't know him as well as you think, or you wouldn't underestimate his scruples and self-control."

Angelique stood, and her eyes glittered with warning. "I don't underestimate him. But I wonder what kind of woman you are, and what you've already done to provoke him."

Caroline clasped her chest dramatically. "Ah. I'm the sleazy Hollywood type on the hunt for instant gratification, you mean?"

"Yes."

"I'm from Beverly Hills. It's a higher level of sleaze."

"Leave him alone!"

Caroline stood as well, drained her milk jauntily, thumped the glass down, and gave Angelique a proud look. "I intend to, but I'm not going to let you turn him into Ward Cleaver."

Angelique interpreted the reference correctly and rolled her eyes. "I'll take that challenge." She stuck out her hand. "This is war, sleazy."

Caroline stared at her for a moment, then smiled thinly. The little darling had guts, and she admired that. "War, June."

They shook hands.


Paul watched Angelique with worried eyes as she bustled around the kitchen, a checkered apron over her ruffled gingham dress. She looked cute, fluffy, and ready for a square dance. That struck him as a tad odd. It was only seven A.M.

"Since when do you like to cook big breakfasts, Angie? I remember you telling Chris that they were bad for his figure."

He spoke to her in French, though it was a colorful Cajun dialect that a Paris native would barely comprehend. She answered the same way, her voice lilting and sweet. "I know how much you like omelets, so I thought this once wouldn't hurt. Besides, it's okay for a man to put on a little weight when he gets older."

Mark wiggled atop his makeshift child's seat, a stack of veterinary books Paul had placed in his chair. "Look, *Maman.* Kitties!"

All four of Paul's enormous cats had leapt to the open window above the sink. They lounged on the sill, gazing hungrily at a ceramic bowl full of omelet mix and sniffing toward the sweet scent of beignets baking in the oven.

"Mornin', purrs," Paul told them amicably.

He glimpsed Angelique as she frowned. She hadn't allowed animals in her and Chris's home, Paul recalled. It was one of many small but disturbing things he kept remembering about her. Why? Why in hell did Angelique, one of his oldest and dearest friends, make him feel suffocated now?

"Shoo!" She picked up a glass of water and tossed it at them before Paul could protest. The cats jackknifed like addled crawfish, but instead of fleeing they bolted onto the kitchen counter.

Tabby slammed into the omelet mix and sent the bowl crashing into the sink, while White Kitty galloped across a pan full of beignets that sat cooling on the stovetop.

Angelique grasped her throat in horror. "They're crazy!"

Paul vaulted to his feet, gazing at his normally sedate cats with astonishment and a guilty desire to laugh. He spread his arms grandly and yelled, "Scram, purrs!"

His booming voice caused Orange to do a major-league slide into a pitcher of grapefruit juice. It sailed off the kitchen counter, and Orange followed it in a bellyflop that ended atop Wolf, who'd been lying on the floor by Mark's chair.

Wolf jumped up, stepped into a puddle of juice, and did an undignified split. He scrambled to a corner, threw his head back, and barked at Orange nonstop, sounding more like his retriever mother than his wolf father.

Blackie leapt for the table edge, caught the yellow and white tablecloth Angelique had put out specially, and hung there in cartoonish dismay showing only eyes, ears, and paws.

Paul stared at him as he slowly sank out of sight, dragging the tablecloth with him. Despite the carnage, the slapstick was too funny to resist. Paul began to laugh.

"Th-th-th-that's all, folks."

Mark squealed with delight while his mother chased cats with a dishcloth. The door to Caroline's room opened and she stepped out, radiating trendy elegance in a green sundress with matching sunglasses and high-heeled granny boots.

She'd plaited her red-gold hair atop her head and wound a green scarf through the braids. Her wide pewter necklace and bracelet were inset with faux emeralds the size of quarters.

Paul inhaled sharply. This was the woman who ought to look foreign to him, yet he craved the sight of her. The cats crashed to a stop around her feet.

"Good morning," she told the disheveled felines cheerfully. "It's the fab four, or would that be the kamikaze kids?"

"Out! Get them out of here!" Angelique told Paul.

He was lost in looking at Caroline and trying to piece together answers to questions he hadn't fully formed yet. There was something odd about her lack of surprise over the scene outside her room. She smiled tolerantly at the cats, grinned at Mark, then smiled at Angelique and received a curt glare in response.

She made a lighthearted kissing gesture at him as she glided through the mess and out the door to the main hallway.

Wolf and all four cats trotted after her calmly, tails up.

Mark slapped both hands over his mouth and giggled. "I know a secret," he announced again.

It was difficult not to like a person who remained so cheerful despite being attacked by cats, ducks, and squirrels.

Caroline scowled as she sat down under a tree and waited to put Wolf through his paces in the next scene. Thankfully the hubbub of the set distracted everyone from noticing her. She needed a minute to keep reminding herself that she was trying to drive Angelique away only for Paul's sake.

The ducks had been a grand ploy, even better than the attack cats at breakfast, but not, Caroline thought happily, as good as the squirrels who dropped nuts on Angelique's head during her picnic lunch with Paul. The woman was trying to feed him into a stupor.

Caroline smiled wickedly. Angelique hadn't crossed paths with the llamas yet.

"Caroline."

Paul's voice made her jump. Feeling a little guilty, Caroline tilted her head back and squinted up at more than six feet of incredibly provocative masculinity in a white polo shirt, comfortable-looking tan trousers, and loafers. From that angle he made her feel even more overwhelmed than usual.

"Clean and nicely dressed again," she teased awkwardly. "Twice in three weeks. Is this a record?"

He dropped to his heels beside her and studied her with narrowed eyes, his expression stern.

As always, the sudden closeness of those searing blue eyes and his expressive, offbeat features made her feel giddy inside. How could she ever describe him to anyone and do him justice?

*His nose is a little big and his hair's two inches too long in back. Mother Nature gave him the kind of strong features that belong on an old Roman coin. He's not the least bit pretty. But he's the sexiest man in this universe.*

"Yes?" she inquired politely.

"Mark keeps saying that you told him secrets. Angie is kind of upset because he won't say what they are. Do you know what he's talkin' about?"

Giddiness turned to anxiety. She didn't want to call Mark an overimaginative little boy again; it wasn't fair to put that onus on him. "Angelique doesn't like me, and she just doesn't want me to talk to him."

"Angie's not suspicious or petty. Why wouldn't she like you?"

Caroline winced. It was true—Angelique didn't seem like the vindictive sort. She wasn't the kind of woman who would, for example, tell squirrels to drop nuts on another woman.

Honesty was the antidote for guilt. "She thinks I'm chasing you, doc."

A slow look of surprise crept into his expression. "She said so?"

"Yes. And I told her that I wasn't."

His mouth thinned. "Thanks."

"But I didn't give her carte blanche to turn you into a couch potato either."

He tilted his head to one side and looked bewildered. "What?"

Caroline put a reassuring hand on his forearm. The thick, corded muscles flexed at her touch; the black hair was smooth and soft in contrast. Even that innocent contact seemed to electrify the air between them. A primitive awareness flickered in his eyes.

She pretended not to notice. "Don't get involved with her a second time, doc. Let her remember how good the past was, but don't promise her the future."

His voice was gruff. "Why?"

"Would you kiss her the way you've kissed me—like you wanted sex and danger and affection all rolled into one? Be honest, now. I won't use it against you."

Even his deep olive skin was capable of blushing, she noticed. It was endearing to see that a man with so much self-confidence could react this way. But he didn't look embarrassed, just caught.

"You've got a way of puttin' things, *chère*."

"Well? Would you?"

"All right. No."

Caroline quivered inside. His skin was growing hot under her fingers. "Then you don't want to marry her. I know she's a bundle of sweetness and compatibility, but she'll either tame you or bore you—either way it wouldn't be very good."

"And who *would* be good for me, huh?" he asked grimly.

"Find someone who appreciates you for what you are." She smiled to diffuse the tension. "A wild and exasperating pain in the butt."

He looked at her sardonically. "Hey, don't let anyone ever tell you that you don't know how to compliment a man."

"I mean it, Blue. Don't let your domestic urges fool you. You may be a practical man, but you don't want a practical marriage."

He was beginning to get angry; she could see it in the tightening of his jaw. "You're damned arrogant to coach me on how to have a happy love life."

"I'm an expert on unhappy love lives."

"I think it's your one talent," he retorted. The stricken look on her face made him curse darkly. His voice softened with apology. "Just mind your own business, Caroline."

"Okay. I deserved that." She dropped her grip on his

arm and looked away, trying desperately to hide her distress.

He clamped one big hand onto her shoulder, shook her slightly, and muttered in a troubled tone, "What you need is the right man to carry you off someplace and make love to you until you can't think about anything but him."

Caroline almost blurted out that she thought a certain Cajun hellion was the only man capable of doing that job. She bit the words back and said instead, "Write me up a prescription, doc. I'll try to get it filled."

He smiled wearily at her joke and left her sitting there, her hands curled limply in her lap, her face flushed, her eyes following him with desperate devotion.

The last thing Caroline wanted to do was get any of the animals in trouble, and especially not Wolf. But in the end, Wolf's own intuition ruined her plan.

Angelique spent the afternoon on the perimeter of the set, where Caroline would be sure to see her. She carried a camera and gathered pictures—pictures of Paul with Mark in his arms, Paul kneeling beside Wolf, Paul with the actors, and, each time she could snare a passerby to do the honors, Paul with Angelique.

Caroline gritted her teeth and guided Wolf through his last scene. Frederick lay on the ground, ailing from some mysterious malady only the film's scriptwriters understood. Wolf lay beside him, looking woebegone and licking Frederick's cosmetically grizzled face.

Considering Wolf's dislike for Frederick and vice versa, they were both consummate professionals, Caroline thought.

The scene went beautifully. Everyone cheered when the director called, "That's like, a take, you know. Let's chill out for the day. No work tomorrow. Like have a great Sunday, okay?"

Caroline looked off the set, hoping to see Paul's approval, and instead found him posing with Mark, Angelique, and Frank while a makeup woman snapped their picture.

The woman set the camera down on a folding chair and went to degrizzle Frederick. Angelique grasped Frank's hands and engaged him in a conversation that made him smile. Paul listened over her shoulder, and *he* smiled.

Caroline squinted at the happy scene in dismay. Dammit, all this sweetness was too much. Frank hardly ever smiled.

Wolf brushed past Caroline's knees at a lope. He barely paused as he snatched Angelique's camera into his mouth. When Paul whistled for him to return, he kept going, straight for the woods, where he disappeared without looking back.

Caroline took one look at the anger in Paul's eyes and knew that Wolf wouldn't go unpunished. Not that Paul would hit him; he never laid a hand on any of the animals at Grande Rivage, no matter how ornery.

A zebra had told her that.

Her stomach knotting, Caroline ran to Paul's group. Angelique had a why-me-Lord? expression on her face. Frank was nonplussed—nothing Wolf did surprised him anymore. Mark gazed at everyone with a child's fascination for impending trouble between adults.

"I'll get your camera back," Caroline assured Angelique.

Paul turned toward her and asked with grim accusation, "Why, did you tell Wolf to take it?"

Caroline stared at him in astonishment. "You think I . . ." Wolf had only been reacting to her disgust for the camera. She couldn't blame him. "It was a joke, Paul."

"You wanted to hurt Angelique."

"No."

He shook his head. "Don't act sorry. You're not."

She felt his disappointment so keenly that she didn't

care that Angelique was watching with a prim, victorious smile.

Caroline wavered. "It was a thoughtless joke."

Paul scowled at her. "I never knew you could be petty or mean," he said in a carefully controlled voice. "Until now. You owe Angie an apology."

His words cut into her as nothing had in years, but she faced Angelique with quiet honor. "I apologize. It was a poor joke."

"It wasn't a joke, Caroline," Paul insisted. "And you know it."

"Oh, Blue, I'm sure she was just trying to show off Wolf's training," Angelique said in a magnanimous tone.

Paul's harsh gaze never left Caroline's contrite one. "No, Angie, you don't understand. Caroline enjoys making fun of other people. Especially people who're different from her. You can't be nice to her, 'cause she doesn't know how to return it."

"I, uhmm, I'll go get Wolf," Caroline murmured, knowing that her rigid facial muscles couldn't stand the strain of holding back her misery much longer. She deserved his anger, but he had no idea how defeated and alone it made her feel.

He was wrong in his assessment of her motives, but telling him so would sound only like a whimpering excuse at this point. Besides, he'd probably marry Angelique and be happy in a way she'd envy, even if it were only a modest happiness.

"You move out of my house," he added softly. "Tonight. Frank'll have to find you someplace else to stay."

Caroline couldn't drag a response from her throat without crying, so she simply nodded.

"I think you're teaching Wolf things that can only get him in trouble. He's working fine now. You can go back to California. Tomorrow."

"Paul, now, wait a minute," Frank interjected somberly.

Caroline swallowed hard and knew that Paul watched

every second of her effort. This last blow had destroyed her defenses. "I never had . . . a client like . . . Wolf before," she managed to say in a choked, quivering voice that gave away all her desperation. "At least don't take him away from me . . . please."

The anger wavered in his eyes, and they filled with a sheen of frustration and anguish. He looked down quickly, a muscle flexing in his jaw as he struggled to get his emotions under control.

"All right," he said between clenched teeth. "Just get your stuff out of my house. And keep away from Angie and Mark."

"That isn't necessary," Angelique said.

Caroline trembled with mortification. Nothing was worse than being defended by June Cleaver.

"I like Caroline," Mark interceded in a tearful voice. "She wouldn't hurt anybody. She's *not* mean. She even lets a granddaddy longlegs live in her room."

Caroline blinked rapidly and dug her fingernails into her palms. *Oh, Mark, you sweetheart.* If she stayed here another second she'd gush more water than a fire hydrant.

"I'll get Wolf."

"I want him chained up in one of the barns tonight," Paul told her, his voice still soft with strain. "That way he'll stay out of trouble until Angie and Mark leave tomorrow. Take him to Ed and tell him I said so."

"Have a heart, Paul," Frank urged.

"Stay out of this, *ami*. Run your movie and let me run my plantation."

"Please don't chain Wolf up," Caroline begged. She grasped Paul's arm. "You'll hurt him more than you'll ever hurt me by doing that."

"How do you know?" he demanded hoarsely. "Eh? Just how do you know?"

"She talks to the animals," Mark said fervently. "Inside their heads."

"Mark, stop pretending!" Angelique ordered.

Paul swiveled toward the child. "What do you mean, *petit?*"

"Don't chain Wolf up," Caroline asked again. "I'll keep him with me. What he did wasn't his fault."

Distracted by her plea, Paul forgot his question to Angelique's son. "Wolf knows better." He slashed the air with one hand. "This crazy discussion is closed."

"Why don't you chain me up instead? I'm the one you're so eager to punish."

His eyes were guarded and fathomless. "Wolf can learn different. You're hopeless."

"Please, don't."

He looked past her. "Wolf! *Venez!*"

Wolf trotted out of the woods, his nose covered in dirt from burying the offending camera. Caroline watched him come straight for Paul without any sign of shrinking.

*Wolf. He thinks we're very bad. Go away while I explain.*

*Wolf won't disobey Master again.*

He sat down in front of Paul and looked up solemnly. Paul gestured from him to Caroline. "Go." He turned toward her and ordered, "Take him to Ed."

Caroline shook her head and said in a broken tone, "I can't do it."

"Then I will."

*Chain!* Wolf communicated in alarm as he caught the drift of her thoughts. His ears drooped and he whined.

Paul winced at that heartrending reaction, but he snapped his fingers and strode toward the barns. Wolf crept alongside him but glanced back at Caroline repeatedly.

*How were we very bad?*

*Wolf. I'm sorry. I was bad. Not you. Master is angry with me.*

Puzzlement. *Lick his nose. He'll know you like him. It's not that easy with people.*
*What is that under your eyes?*
*That's sadness.*

There was a potent pause as Wolf turned his gaze up to Paul's face. *Master has it under his eyes too.*

Paul sat in a big rocking chair on the front veranda, surrounded by a private darkness that suited his mood, and watched a new moon over the edge of the trees. His senses dull with unhappiness, he wasn't certain how long he had been there when he heard the soft crunch of feet on gravel.

He looked to his left and saw a tall, loose-limbed shadow ambling up the walkway that ran past the house toward the outbuildings.

"*Bonjour*, doc," Frank called jovially. Frank breezed onto the veranda, gave a totally uncharacteristic hoot of laughter, and slumped down in a rocker beside Paul's.

"I had hoped to find you awake, my man, so that I might chat with you in private." Frank enunciated his words as if every consonant mattered.

"Frank, my man, you're soused."

"I have had a drop more than my Saturday night cocktail, 'tis true. Sir Frederick and I were playing cards and drinking bourbon with your college interns. A mighty challenge, those youngsters."

Paul leaned back in his rocker and shut his eyes. "This isn't like you, Frank."

"I'm rather perturbed, I admit it. I've been wrestling with my personal creed. The one about not meddling in other people's personal creeds."

Paul looked at him wearily. "Frank, I'll fix you a cup of strong coffee, yes?"

"No." Frank shook his head and rocked with vigor.

"Slow down, Captain Kirk, you're about to reach warp speed."

"Oh." Frank brought the chair to a halt. "As the Walrus said to the something-or-other, 'I have come to talk of many things, of cabbages and sailing ships, of Caroline and . . .' Whoops. Did I say Caroline?"

Paul got up and leaned against one of the veranda's columns. "Where is she?"

"She is in the barn, in the stall where Wolf is chained, sitting in the hay with his head in her lap. She is reading an Agatha Christie novel to him, and he seems to be enjoying it."

"Are my cats there too?"

"Yes, indeed. I think they're bored by Christie. They're all asleep." Frank cleared his throat. "You hurt Carrie today, my man. More than you can ever imagine."

Inside his pockets Paul's hands clenched into fists. "Tell me everything you know about her. Help me understand her."

"Ah." Frank slapped the arms of his chair. "Here's where I fought my personal creed to a standstill. What do you want to know?"

"Did she really love your brother?"

"Ah. Tom and Caroline. Let me tell you a little story, my friend. Tom introduced me to Caroline five years ago. Here was this young woman, twenty-one years old at the time, I think, a hard-nosed runaway from Connecticut who'd spent the last four years living in San Francisco with a Chinese family. They'd given her a job in their restaurant, then a place in their home, and she'd practically become a member of their family."

Paul frowned in the darkness. "When she told me that she left home at seventeen I thought she meant she'd gone to live with some friends."

"No. She had nothing and no one. Does that help you understand why she learned to be so tough? Anyhow, she was the new kennel attendant at a ritzy place where Tom boarded his goofy Airedale. Damned dog hated everyone but Tom. The dog fell over and licked Caroline's feet, Caroline hugged the dog, and then she says to Tom, 'He's just lonely. If you buy him a puppy to keep him company, he'll be perfectly fine.' "

Frank chortled. "And she was right. By then Tom was just as smitten with her as his dog was. Anyhow, he brought her over to meet me because he thought she could help me with an ornery skunk I'd hired for a TV show. Skunk was mean as hell, but we had to have him. She goes off with the skunk for ten minutes, comes back and says, 'Spray him with Chanel No. 5.' We did. Skunk's in ecstasy. A joy to deal with from then on."

"And about Tom?" Paul asked in exasperation.

"So people in the industry heard about the skunk, and she started to get other jobs. Pretty soon she had her own animal consulting business. The rest is history."

"And Tom?"

"Oh. When I first met her I thought, 'What does this tough-talking, arrogant kid want with a shy, strait-laced accountant who has severe diabetes?' And you know what she wanted?"

"What?" Paul held his breath.

"To take care of him."

*"What?"*

"She'd never had anybody to take care of. And no-body to take care of her. And, by God, she treated him like a king. She made him sublimely happy, and he returned the favor. She was hell on the rest of the world until Tom softened her up and we finally realized that she was just scared to death of us. You may not believe this right now, but to know Caroline is to love Caroline."

Paul puzzled over her past. "She was faithful to Tom?"

"Without a doubt."

"But after he died, she was lonely, yes?"

"Sure. She lived with Gretchen and me for a while until she got over his death."

"No, I mean, then she started dating again. Okay, who does she have now? What's his name? What are *their* names? Tell me the truth, Frank."

After a silent moment Frank said softly, "This is where my personal creed against meddling takes a real nosedive." He stood up proudly, as if surrendering in good conscience after fighting a noble battle.

"There isn't anyone and hasn't been anyone in the two years since Tom died."

Paul stared at him in the darkness. "No one? She didn't go back to California to see somebody?"

Frank sighed grandly. "My friend, you are dealing with a rarity: a one-man woman who's been waiting for that one man. And you're him."

# *Seven*

Caroline woke up to the sound of rustling straw, the hot puff of Wolf's breath against her arm, and the sharp tugging of his teeth in the sleeve of her pink T-shirt.

"Hmmm?" She rubbed eyes swollen from intermittent crying, shifted her aching shoulders against the stall's coarse partition, then checked her wristwatch and saw that midnight had just passed. "I'm sorry. I always fall asleep when I read in bed."

*She-friend is back. Help me go. Help me.*

Caroline tossed the Agatha Christie book out of her lap and grasped Wolf's ruff. His gaze burned into her and he poked her leg with one huge gray paw. *How do you know?* she asked.

*I feel it.*

*Where is she-friend?*

*A long way. But I can get there.*

*Oh, Wolf. Wait until morning. Then I'll ask Master if you can go.*

He jumped over her outstretched legs and lunged frantically against the thick chain that ran from his leather collar to an iron ring in the wall. Caroline scrambled to her feet and tried to stroke his head. The cats, curled in the straw around him, jumped up amid the commotion and ran.

*Help me, help me,* Wolf begged. *She needs me.*

His desperation overwhelmed Caroline, and she quickly unbelted his collar. Wolf bolted out the open stall door.

"Wait! I'll go with you!" Caroline called, but he was already racing past the curious heads of Paul's quarter horse brood mares. He shoved through the unlatched door at the end of the barn's wide corridor and disappeared into the night.

*Don't put sadness under your eyes. I'll come back.*

Caroline ran to the end of the corridor and stood for several minutes, gazing after Wolf in open-mouthed dismay. Paul would never forgive her for turning Wolf loose, and she certainly couldn't tell him why she'd done it.

*You see, doc, I talked with him and he said he had to go help his girlfriend. That was the reason he's been depressed.*

Her shoulders slumped. It was better to suffer anger than disbelief, she thought wearily. She'd learned that lesson long ago.

Caroline walked numbly back into the stall and sank down on her sleeping bag. While preparing for a night of keeping Wolf company she'd exchanged her sundress for loose green chinos, the pink T-shirt, and her jogging shoes. Caroline drew her knees up, hooked her hands around them, and gazed blankly at the wall across from her.

When Paul learned that she'd set Wolf free against his wishes, he'd send her away from Grande Rivage for good, and neither Frank nor anyone else would be able to change his mind. An emptiness like nothing she'd known before grew inside her as she thought about leaving him and his wonderful home.

A few minutes later she heard the barn door swing open. Caroline stiffened with dread; she absorbed the horses' affectionate, welcoming attitude and knew who'd just entered the building.

She shut her eyes and groaned silently. Paul had come to check on Wolf.

Caroline gazed at the empty collar lying in the straw and strained to pick up his footsteps on the hallway's sawdust floor. Finally he reached the stall door and stopped. She looked up wretchedly and found a stunned expression on his face.

"What have you done now?" he asked, but with less anger than she'd expected.

"I turned him loose. He'll be back."

Paul stepped inside the stall and dropped to his heels by the collar. He fingered it thoughtfully, frowning. Caroline gazed at him with bittersweet sorrow, part of her mind focused only on her problem and part focused solely on the heart-stirring sight he presented in old jeans and a soft white pullover, his thick black hair feathering over the ribbed neckline in back.

In Angelique's honor he'd traded his lace-up work boots for loafers all weekend. A significant sacrifice, Caroline thought enviously. He really cared about that woman and her son—and why shouldn't he? They were terrific.

He raised his head and studied her intensely. "Why did you disobey my orders about Wolf?"

Her heart racing, Caroline pretended to study a seam on her pants. "He was miserable. And since you couldn't be any more disgusted with me than you already are, what difference does it make?"

"I'm not disgusted with you." He met her shocked gaze and held it. "*Chère,* I need answers."

Caroline inhaled raggedly. He hadn't called her by that endearment in some time, and never in such a loving voice before. A hunger for more flashed through her veins. "Answers?" she echoed in a high, innocent tone.

"You're not going to make it easy, no. I can tell. You're too worried that things won't work out. I understand."

Confused and feeling trapped by her reckless greed for his affection and approval, she braced her hands in the hay and sidled back against the wall. "I'm glad you understand, because I don't."

Moving slowly, he knelt in front of her. The dim overhead light bulb cast inky shadows on his hair and drew mysterious emotions on his face. That couldn't be affection and approval she saw. The shadows played tricks on her. All her life the shadows had played tricks.

"You belong here," he told her in a low, firm voice. "At Grande Rivage. You belong with me."

"No," she said, shaking her head desperately.

He grasped at the air with one hand, catching invisible problems. "Your memories about your mother," he murmured. His hand moved again. "Your distrust of your Cajun heritage. Your insecurity about your scar. Your fears about wanting me, a man who lives a lifestyle that's very different from yours."

With one dramatic gesture Paul flung the problems away. "*Allez*. Poof." He shook his head slowly, his eyes on hers, then touched his forefinger over her heart. "This is all that's important." He brought his finger to a spot over his own heart.

His eyes became possessive and even more determined. "You can run from yourself, yes, but you can't run from me anymore."

Caroline trembled. She shut her eyes in an attempt to dilute his effect, only to inhale the erotic, purely masculine scent of his skin and hair. It mingled with good, homey aromas—he loved to cook chicken over hickory chips in an old stone grill outside the mansion's back veranda, and she knew from his scent that it was what he'd fixed for dinner tonight.

Hickory smoke and the sweet smell of hay—she'd never smell either again without remembering Paul and this moment. Caroline winced. And she'd remember Angelique, for whom he'd cooked dinner.

"Go away," she begged. He settled closer, rested his big hands atop her knees, and spread his fingers as if she were a button accordion he could play at will. She pressed her head against the wall and turned her face away from him. "Why are you doing this?" she demanded hoarsely.

Every night noise seemed amplified, every movement of the horses' hooves and every rustle of the straw was a vibrant entity because of her aroused and worried state.

"Why did you let me think you had other men when there weren't any, hmmm?" he asked in his soft Cajun patois, as smooth as the underside of a magnolia blossom.

Her stomach knotted. *Frank, you traitor.* "Don't be misled. I'm no shrinking violet where men are concerned."

"For three years you hardly left Tom Windham's side. You had only one man, *chère.* And since he died two years ago, you haven't had a man at all. Why didn't you tell me the truth about why you went back to California the other weekend?"

His warm breath caressed her face. She shut her eyes. "I was trying to keep you from liking me."

"Because you don't want me?" he asked slyly.

Caroline stared at him, her chest rising swiftly. "Just the opposite, and you know it." His face was so near to hers that she could have nuzzled her nose to his. She was awfully tempted to bite it first.

He made a petting motion with one hand. "Easy, easy. I just needed to hear you say so."

Her mouth went dry from nervousness. This was a totally unexpected turn of events; she was no good at handling people at close range, not people who meant a great deal to her, and especially not this assertive Cajun.

"Angelique would be good for you," she announced. "Maybe I misjudged her."

He began to brush a fingertip across her kneecaps. "She's a wonderful woman. And Mark is a great kid. When did you tell him that you had a pet spider in your room?"

"Well, maybe after lunch, no, let's see—"

"I don't remember you having any chance to talk to him after lunch. I don't remember you having any chance to talk to him at all. This is one of the mysteries I'll have to figure out about you. It'll be fun."

Caroline shifted her knees, trying to escape the disastrous trail of sensation his hands sent slipping up and down her legs. "Stop it," she ordered softly. "Go back to the house. Just because you've realized that I have the love life of a rock doesn't mean that anything else has changed. I'm leaving for California when the movie's finished. Don't forget it."

"Hmmm-mm." He cupped his hand over one knee and curled his fingers along the inside.

"Doc, *please*," she begged. "Go back to the house and do something smart. Play your accordion for Angelique."

"She wouldn't have me if I tried."

Caroline gaped at him for a second. "What happened? Did you sic the cats on her again?"

He lifted a black brow. "That's more your territory, eh, witch?"

She shook her head solemnly, and was perturbed to see his eyes crinkle with amused disbelief. He patted the inside of her knee. "I'll figure you out eventually. There's plenty of time."

"No, there's not."

His teasing look faded. "Angie's leaving early in the morning. We had a talk after that mess with the camera this afternoon. She said she saw things between you and me that I can't ignore."

Unable to speak without her voice breaking, Caroline squinted at him and tried to look nonplussed.

He moved his fingertips in lazy circles, making tingles run down the muscles of her legs. "I thought you just wanted anything that was Cajun to be your joke—especially me," he continued, his tone low and apologetic. "I thought that you were laughing at me for being old-fashioned."

Tenderness burst inside her. "I was envying you. And trying to protect you from making a mistake with Angelique." She paused, grimaced with the effort of revealing her motives to herself as well as to Paul, then finally admitted, "And I was trying to drive my competition away."

He bent his head to her knees. "It tore me up when I realized that I'd humiliated you for caring about me, *chère*. I won't ever do it again."

Tears flooded her eyes. She pressed her fingertips to the corners. "Cut it out, doc. I don't deal with kindness real well."

"You'll have to learn." He grasped her by the shoulders. Caroline lifted her head just as he leaned forward, and suddenly he was kissing her, his mouth a gentle, possessive force that made her whimper with pleasure.

His tongue stroked hers for a moment, the action meant to soothe but also to excite. Caroline wound her fingers into his shirt and sagged forward, giving herself to his delicious mixture of sweetness and passion.

He pushed her knees apart and moved within the boundaries of her legs, then slid his hands down to her hips. He sat back and lifted her to his lap.

Still lost in his intimate, ever-changing kiss, Caroline straddled his thighs, her knees hugging them on either side. She draped her arms around his neck and drew away from his seductive mouth just enough to dab urgent kisses across his lips.

She saw her own desire reflected in his half-shut eyes and flushed face. Just looking at him made her quiver from restraint; the squeezing pressure of his hands on her rump was an enticement as old as time, and she wanted to surround him, to let her hips arch against him while his hands urged her on.

"This is why people do crazy, foolish things," she murmured brokenly. "This feeling. I finally understand how people can claim that nothing else matters."

He tilted his head and gave her one of his solemn, endearing looks of bewilderment. "Don't make it sound so terrible."

Caroline rested her forehead against his. For a moment her mind remained in a haze, every nerve ending geared to the scent and feel of him. Her fingers itched to explore the expanse of hard, muscled shoulders under his shirt; her face tingled as she imagined herself rubbing catlike along the hint of beard on his jaw.

"I don't want to hurt or disappoint you," she said plaintively. "I'll leave this place tonight rather than take that chance."

"I'd just come after you. Shhh. I'm a big ol' tough man with a hide like a 'gator's, yes? Don't worry about me."

She shook him lightly. "I can't stay in Louisiana, Blue. There are too many bad memories, and I'd live in dread of running across my mother's family one day."

"Shhh. Why try to answer all the questions before the test starts?"

He pulled her forward a little, then lay back on the straw and smiled at her wickedly.

Caroline gasped as his tactic brought her feverish center into direct contact with the rising bulge inside his trousers. He held her hips still and arched gently against her.

"You're seducing me against my will," she whispered, her eyes heavy with desire and her voice husky. "I thought this kind of thing could happen only in my imagination."

"If we weren't lying here where anyone could walk up and catch us, I'd give your imagination an even bigger jolt."

"This is . . . new. I feel *new*." She gestured vaguely, then let her hands fall to his chest.

His breath short, his eyes tender but questioning, he relaxed underneath her. He reached up and cupped her chin. "*Chère*, what does sex mean to you?"

Caroline blinked in surprise, and a chill of regret ran through her. She looked at him worriedly. Understanding filled his expression, and he grasped her arms.

"Come here. Beside me," he asked, pulling her down.

With a troubled sigh she snuggled into the harbor of his shoulder and hugged one arm over his chest. He languidly caressed her face, and she was glad that her scar lay hidden against his side.

"What does it mean for you?" he repeated gently. "A few minutes of physical sensation? A way to show love? Or just something to offer so you'll get the affection you need?"

Caroline shut her eyes. "The last one. At least that's the way it was until I turned seventeen—when I ran away from home. I learned a lot about sex and nothing about love."

Paul's hand never faltered. He touched her hair, stroked it gently, and tightened his arm around her shoulders. "That was your stepparents' fault."

His attitude and gentleness scattered her worries. Caroline exhaled shakily. "I'm just being honest with you. I was nobody's angel. I wanted to embarrass my stepparents and thumb my nose at all the average, regular, *happy* kids my age."

She shook her head. "So I dated the bad guys, the troublemakers—and I did what I thought I had to do to make them like me."

"It's no crime for a mixed-up teenager to make mistakes. I just wanted to know how it had been with you."

"Oh, doc," she whispered. "Doc." Her tears dampened his shoulder. Caroline admitted silently that she loved this sweetheart of a man. No matter what distances might separate them, no matter what happened to their mismatched pairing, she loved him.

She made a soft keening sound of devotion and turned her face toward his chest. "Later, when I was older, it was different with Tom," she murmured.

"I figured that, yes."

"He taught me how to care. Everything he did was unselfish. There weren't any fireworks with Tom, but I didn't mind."

Paul twisted his head and kissed her hair. "So you went from one extreme to the other." His deep voice was a little coy. "How would you like to try a mixture, hmmm? Sex *and* romance?"

Caroline's heart clattered in her chest. "Sounds lovely, but I'm not sure I'd know how to act."

"You'll learn."

"I should pack my fanny onto the next plane for California. For your sake as well as mine. Getting involved is not as simple as you want it to be," she protested.

He shook his head and chuckled. " 'Tis too, *chère*."

"You're forgetting that I can truly be a bitch at times."

"And I can truly be a bastard."

"No, you're a hellion. That's much nicer."

"Well then, you're no worse than a hellion either."

Caroline began to smile helplessly. She knew deep down that they were headed for some devastating decisions, but that realization couldn't overwhelm the sweet sense of happiness growing inside her chest.

She cuffed one of Paul's ears playfully. "We've never had a good, long conversation about regular stuff. Maybe we can't do it."

"Like what stuff?"

She thought for a moment, her hand curling and uncurling in his shirt. "Favorite movies, books, foods, etcetera."

"*The Day the Earth Stood Still*, any mystery by Dick Francis, and seafood."

Caroline huffed drolly. "Not bad. I like those things too."

"Let's have a date. Right now. We'll stay here all night and get to know each other."

"A date?"

He tickled her cheek with his fingertips. "It's one of those romantic things where a man and a woman talk to each other without arguing or making love."

She smiled tentatively. "Are you sure we can manage that?"

"Let's give it a try, *chère*."

Feeling giddy, Caroline propped herself on one elbow and stuck a piece of straw in her mouth at a jaunty angle. Tenderness and affection coursed through her like a fine wine as she looked at the gentle barbarian sprawled next to her, his expression absurdly prim.

Caroline smiled at him and was rewarded by a searing look of affection. For the first time in her life, she felt very much at home.


Angelique left the next morning with great dignity and a handshake that nearly crushed Caroline's fingers. Her son, unaware of the mood, hugged Caroline good-bye.

"I will," he said.

As soon as Angelique's zippy red subcompact disappeared at the end of the long oak corridor, Paul turned to Caroline and asked, "Will what?"

She laughed to hide her awkwardness. "He thinks I can read his mind."

Paul grinned widely and shook his head. "Kids live in a great fantasy world."

"Yeah." As Paul took her hand and led her to the house for breakfast, Caroline fought a twinge of guilt over her deception. She'd never told Tom about her gift, so why should she tell Paul?

Because Tom didn't inhabit your soul the way Paul does, she told herself.

"Sleepy?" he asked after they filled up on sugary beignets and pungent cappuccino.

"I don't know." Caroline clasped her wrist as if testing her pulse. "Sugar and caffeine level are at maximum, Captain. She's ready for warp speed."

Paul slapped the kitchen table exuberantly. "You're a *Star Trek* fan. Me too."

Caroline laughed. "That's probably the only thing we didn't discuss last night. My voice sounds like a croak."

"No, it's very Lauren Bacall."

Caroline sighed. "You adore me. Such good taste."

"Then you won't mind swinging with me."

"Eh, Tarzan?"

"In the hammock. Out back. Big enough for two."

"Two what?"

He stood, jerked a thumb toward the back veranda, and smiled wickedly. "Move your *petit cul.*"

"When I find out what a *cul* is, I hope I'm pleased."

"That was a compliment, and yours is great."

Holding hands, they strolled out into a pleasant fall morning with air washed clean by a dawn shower. Insects chorused in the honeysuckle and magnolias beyond the backyard; the moss glistened on oaks still silver with moisture.

Paul took her to a huge hammock strung between two of the trees. "I've always intended to see if swinging in a hammock was fun," she commented.

"No hammocks in California?"

"Nah. Just swingers. No hammocks."

Chuckling, Paul picked her up and laid her in the soft white web. He went to the other side and settled beside her. He crossed his feet at the ankles; she copied him. He put his hands behind his head; she put hers behind her head.

The hammock swung gently, and a fragrant morning breeze curled under Caroline's back. She felt Paul's body pressing against hers from shoulder to calf, cozy and inviting. "Heaven," she whispered.

"See?" he teased. "You do what I do, the world is fine, yes?"

Caroline looked at him, blinked sleepily and happily, and whispered with wistful hope, "Maybe so."

But the world wasn't fine, not when Wolf failed to come home by dusk. Carolines sat on the floor, the flowing skirt of a yellow shirtwaist dress tucked around her legs, and watched Paul pace the big parlor along the front of the house, his footsteps reverberating on the old hardwood boards.

Guilt twisted her stomach. "He'll come back," she offered.

"He never disappeared like this before the movie people came. I don't understand. Maybe he's stressed out, like Frank kept telling me before he brought you here."

"I don't think it has anything to do with the movie." She paused. "Doc, how long have you had Wolf, and how did you get him?"

Lost in thought, Paul distractedly ran his hands over his gray sweatshirt, then sank them into the pockets of his jeans. Caroline watched the languid gathering of shadows around him and the way the fading light caressed his hard-drawn face. Put this man in virtually any environment and he made it hum with sensuality.

Paul gazed at the floor in thought. "I've had Wolf two years last month. Got him from a roadside zoo when he was six weeks old. The bastard who ran it had one of those nasty little tourist traps."

Paul spread his hands as if outlining a sign. " 'See the alligators. See the wolves. Buy your beer, food, gas.' This jerk had a pen with a couple of stagnant puddles full of baby 'gators and a wire cage holding little bitty Wolf, lookin' sick and mean."

Caroline thumped her knees. "I hope you raised hell."

"Yeah, that guy, I got him shut down the next day. I took the 'gators and turned 'em loose. The first night Wolf spends here at the plantation I put him in a box by my bed—you know, with an old blanket and a chew toy. I woke up in the middle of the night with Wolf snuggled under my chin. He knew right from the start that I was his friend."

"He'd die for you." Caroline rested her chin on her knees and shivered from emotion as she watched Paul come to a halt. *I understand why.*

Paul looked at her with troubled, searching eyes. "That stuff Mark said about you talking to the animals. I think you *do* talk to them some how."

Blanching, she fumbled for a reply. The phone rang upstairs in Paul's bedroom, and Caroline exhaled gratefully as he loped out of the parlor to answer it.

A minute later he bounded down the stairs at high speed. "Let's go, Caro," he yelled. "Neighbor of mine has got Wolf hemmed up in his shed. Says Wolf attacked him."

In terms of the secluded bayou land, Paul's neighbor was close by, but it took twenty minutes to reach Andrew Dulac's small, well-kept farm.

Dulac, a paunchy middle-aged man wearing khaki coveralls and rubber boots, came out of a white clapboard house and ambled through the half light as Caroline and Paul climbed out of Paul's truck.

Caroline warily eyed the shotgun Dulac carried in the crook of one elbow, but was reassured when Paul went up to the man and clapped him affectionately on the shoulder.

After Paul introduced her, he and the farmer spoke in animated Cajun French for more than a minute. Dulac repeatedly pointed a hand to his disappearing red hair, then held out one arm to show a jagged tear in the sleeve of his plaid shirt. Caroline seethed with curiosity and vowed to learn some form of French, no matter how rudimentary.

Finally Paul turned toward her, frowning. "Wolf tore Andrew's sleeve and tried to catch him by the hair when he fell down. He's taken a fancy to Andrew's farm dog."

"She's just a little part-shepherd bitch," Dulac said in disgust. "Ugly thing, and not real smart. That Wolf, he's got no taste, tryin' to bite me 'cause I don't want her bred."

Caroline frowned. *She-friend hurts,* Wolf had told her right after she arrived at Grande Rivage. "Is she in season?"

"No, but must be coming in soon," Dulac said. "Why else would Wolf act so crazy?"

"Was he here a few weeks ago?" Paul asked.

"Yeah, I've seen him off and on. Thought he'd get over the hots for her when I took her on vacation with me. Left my brother in charge here while I went to visit my mother's people up in Canada. Just got back."

"And you say you took your dog with you?" Caroline confirmed.

"Yeah."

*She-friend gone. Hope she comes back.*

Paul ran his hands through his hair and left it a ruffled black mane. "Guess it's time I bought him a mate. Been meaning to bring in a female wolf for him."

"Don't be a snob," Caroline said lightly. "Maybe he's already found a mate."

"Oooh, I can't give up Sin," Dulac told her. He grinned. "As in 'ugly as sin.' She's too good at catching rats."

"Where is she?" Caroline asked.

Dulac made a huffing sound. "Hunkered down by the shed where ol' Wolf is. Come on, Doc Blue. Get your wild stud and haul him back home."

Caroline met Paul's gaze. She suspected that something was fishy about this situation, but she held her tongue. They followed Dulac through the grounds to a small white toolshed with a padlocked door.

A slender form lay with her back pressed tightly to one side of the shed. Caroline inhaled sharply as she studied the scruffy, medium-sized female dog who bore a passing resemblance to a German shepherd. Caroline smiled at her.

*Sin. Come here, sweetie.*

Caroline heard Wolf's toenails scraping the shed's inside walls. *Help me. Help her. Help us.* Her throat tightened at the desperate tone.

Sin stood up, studied Caroline with pricked ears, then circumvented both Dulac and Paul to come to her. She limped badly. Caroline held out a hand as Sin sat down by her feet with quiet dignity. Sin nuzzled her fingers and looked up at her with intelligent black eyes.

*Mistress. I hear of you. You help.*

Caroline almost staggered. She'd never dreamed of finding another canine with Wolf's sharp intelligence. Her hand began to shake violently as she peered closer in the failing light and saw the jagged, still-healing wounds running across Sin's nose.

*Ugly and scarred. Just like me.* Sin whined at the fervent emotions that Caroline exuded. Caroline took a deep breath and tried to calm down. "What happened to her?" she asked.

"Aw, she got in a fight with an old dog of my uncle's. Didn't help her looks much."

Caroline stared hard into Sin's eyes. *What hurt you?*

The rush of communication made her head swim. Caroline cupped her hands to her temples and tried to hold back the misery and fury that grew inside her. Lord, this was awful. She wanted to throw up, and fought for breath.

Strong hands grasped her shoulders. "You okay?" Paul asked. "What's the matter?"

She wheeled drunkenly and clutched his shirt with both hands. Looking up at him, Caroline implored, "Buy her for Wolf. Or I'll buy her." She swiveled her head toward Dulac and said as calmly as she could, "How much do you want?"

Dulac gaped at her.

"Caroline." Paul squeezed her shoulders gently. He made his voice low and private. "It's the scars. I know. Shhh."

She shook her head. "Please, Talk him into selling her."

"I'm sorry. I can't sell m'dog," Dulac protested.

Caroline twisted toward the man and was vaguely aware of Paul's arm circling her shoulders in a tight, somewhat rebuking grip.

"Quit jerking us around," she retorted. "Name your price, you bastard. I'll pay."

"Stop it!" Paul's voice was rough as he pulled her around to face him. "You can't talk to people that way down here."

Dulac's mouth thinned and he lifted his chin proudly. "I don't do business with uppity women." He tossed Paul the key to the shed. "There you go, *ami*. Take your wolf. Sin! Get back!"

Caroline looked down into pleading eyes. Sin quivered, got gingerly to her feet, but never stopped looking at her for salvation. *You are our only hope.* Inside the shed Wolf emitted a blood-freezing howl. It was too much.

Caroline turned away from Paul and shook both fists at Dulac. Then she called him half a dozen names that made his jaw drop down to his shirt collar.

Looking stunned, Paul stepped in front of her and grabbed her fists. His gaze could have cut diamonds as he glared into her eyes. "I've known this man for years and he's a good neighbor. You're embarrassing the hell out of me. Either be quiet or I'll put you over my shoulder and haul you back to the truck."

Wolf howled louder; Sin bumped Paul in the leg with her nose and directed a query to Caroline. *Should I bite him?*

*No,* Caroline answered hurriedly. *He's your friend, the same as me.*

"Apologize to Andrew," Paul ordered.

Caroline groaned. She wanted to punch Andrew Dulac's smug mouth. Frustrated because the truth coiled inside her like a deadly snake with no place to strike, she turned her ferocity toward the tall, equally fierce man in front of her.

"Try to carry me out of here, pal, and you'll be wearing your ears for cuff links," she threatened.

Paul's eyes flickered with regret. In one swift movement he pulled her right arm up, bent forward, and carefully shoved one brawny shoulder into her midsection. Caroline found herself hanging upside down over his back. Her voluminous yellow skirt tangled between her legs, and Paul anchored one arm behind her knees.

He started toward the truck, his strides swift and angry. Caroline made a hoarse sound of defeat as she thumped at his unrelenting back.

"I can explain," she said.

"Impossible."

God help me, she thought, while the utter hopelessness of the situation sank in. There was only one thing she could do, and Paul might not ever get over it.

"We've got to take Sin away from here! Dulac uses her as bait to train pit bull terriers to kill!"

Paul halted so quickly that she almost slid off his shoulder. He set her down and stared at her in shock.

"Hey!" Dulac interjected, his voice high and frightened. "Hey, doc, you tell that woman not to accuse me of things like that!"

Paul gazed from her to the white-faced farmer, whose discomposure was evident even in the dim light. "You've never met Andrew before."

She shook her head wearily. "I just know. Trust me."

"She's crazy!" Dulac yelled. "That bleedin' heart *Américaine* bitch is trying to get my dog anyway she can!"

Paul's head snapped up, and he seared Dulac with a lethal gaze. Caroline didn't have to understand French to know that what he said to the farmer in her defense could never be repeated in polite company.

His attention finally swiveled back to her. "What do you know about Andrew? This is a bad accusation. *How* do you know? Who told you?"

Caroline muffled an anguished sob. "He took Sin someplace where people train pit bulls to fight. He and his cronies use dogs like Sin as blood bait." She was shaking so hard that she could barely stand still. "Most of the bait animals don't survive. Most of them are puppies and kittens, or old animals that can't fight. But Sin is smart and tough. She survived."

Caroline wavered until suddenly Paul reached out with both hands and caught her under the elbows. She begged him with her eyes. "Dulac has used her for this before. Usually he keeps her out of sight until she heals. If you check under her coat you'll find scars all over her."

"Nobody's touching my dog!" Dulac cried. "Sin! You get! Get!"

Caroline, tears streaming down her face, shut her eyes and said softly, "Sin, come here and lay down by me."

She studied Paul's incredulous expression as he watched Sin limp to her and settle carefully by her sandaled feet. Breathing roughly, he dropped to his heels and slid his fingers into her coat.

In the background Dulac sputtered and threatened. Caroline knelt beside Paul and watched his hands gently search the dog's body. His earlier expression of astonishment was nothing compared to the one that came over his face now.

Then fury supplanted it. He got to his feet so fast that both Caroline and Sin jumped. Striding toward Dulac, he muttered, "I'm takin' your dog."

"You can't prove anything!" Dulac screamed.

Paul said something vicious in French. Then he went to the shed and split the thin plank door with one well-placed kick.

Wolf shot out and immediately dropped to a deadly crouch, his eyes on Dulac. "No," Paul ordered. "Wolf. *Allez.* There are better ways to settle this."

Caroline wobbled to her feet. *Wolf. It's over. Let's take your mate and go home.*

Wolf snarled at Dulac, stalked over to Paul, shoved his nose into Paul's hand with blunt affection, then came to Caroline and Sin.

His scarred, abused mate whimpered, wagged her tail fervently, and reached up to touch her battered nose to his elegant silver muzzle. Wolf gave her face a gentle lick, then looked at Caroline with solemn dignity.

*Thank you. No more sadness under our eyes.*

# Eight

Darkness had fallen, and light from a lamppost cast long shadows on the truck. Paul noticed that Caroline shifted position so that her face was hidden in them. He got goose bumps at the thought of learning every secret hidden behind her scarred but beautiful mask. Paul lowered the tailgate and held out his arms.

"Come here, sorceress, and bring your apprentices."

Still cuddling Sin on her lap, Caroline studied him with troubled eyes. "Thank you for believing what I said about Dulac. I'm not crazy."

"I didn't say you are." Paul sighed, leaned forward, and braced his hands on the truck bed, his eyes riveted to hers. "Let's you and me have a talk, yes? I want to know what kind of power you have with animals."

Her reaction was immediate and frightened. She stroked Sin's head rapidly, opened her mouth to speak, shut it, looked at Wolf as if searching for help, then finally set Sin off her lap and scrambled to her feet with quick, angry movements.

"Wolf doesn't need my help anymore. I'm going back to California. Tonight." Her voice was icy.

Paul gazed up at her in astonishment at the change from tender to tough. "The hell you are."

"Don't boss me, doc. I'll go get my things together."

She started forward, hesitated awkwardly when she saw that he wasn't about to move out of her way, then hurried to the side of the truck and began to climb over. Her face was constricted with hidden emotion, and she knotted one hand over her stomach in anxiety.

He reached her before she swung her feet to the ground. "Time to face the music, *chère*," he said grimly, and grabbed her by one wrist.

She raged when he slung her facedown over one shoulder and pinned her in place with his arms. Paul staggered into the house while she struggled desperately and burned the air with oaths. By the time he reached the top of the stairs and entered his bedroom he knew that he'd have bruises where her sharp-toed sandals had pummeled his legs and her fists had thudded against his back.

He dropped her in the middle of his bed. "I'll be back after I make my rounds," he told her. "Meantime, you're not goin' anywhere. Get ready to tell me the truth about your hokus-pokus." He added wryly, "And don't call any llamas or cats to rescue you."

She shoved herself into a sitting position, her yellow dress twisted, legs splayed, hair tousled over her eyes like a red-gold curtain, and her mouth ajar at his tactics. Then she yelped with fury. "It won't work. I don't have anything to tell you. I'm just a good animal trainer."

He described that claim with a hearty barnyard epithet as he strode to a heavy teakwood dresser. Paul flicked a lamp on, then pulled a long key from a creaking dresser drawer.

"Love this old house," he said jovially, holding the key aloft for Caroline's perusal. "The bedroom doors lock from the outside."

"Don't!"

"Too late."

He walked out the door, slammed it shut, and turned the key.

Caroline paced. She pounded one fist on the side of an antique oak dresser and kicked one massive leg of his barbarian bed.

*I can't tell him the truth. He'll think I'm a nut.*

Caroline strained her ears, listening to sounds in the rooms below as he returned from making his nightly rounds to check on both animals and staff. Her heart threatened to dent her chest when his footsteps reverberated on the staircase.

She walked numbly to a window and stood with her back to the door, hugging herself. Chills ran down her spine when the key rattled in the lock. Caroline stared resolutely into the night.

Paul stepped into the room and shut the door. His voice came to her, low and firm, but pleasant. "Relax, *chère*, and come here."

"I want out of this room." Caroline stiffened even more and kept gazing into the night.

"Nope."

She stifled a cry of dismay as she heard the key turning once more in the lock. There were other sounds then—soft, creaking ones—and she realized that Paul had settled on his bed.

"Got a bottle of wine and a bowl of seafood gumbo here," he offered politely. "Got a comfortable place to sit. Shame if you don't share with me."

Caroline swung about angrily, her hands clenched. He sat on the bed with one leg dangling casually over the side, a tray containing the gumbo and wine set in front of him on the thick, multicolored quilt. The light of the lamp placed him half in shadow and half out, making the whole scene disastrously intimate.

*The barbarian king had come to claim his prisoner.*

She shivered and fought a knot of despair in her throat. "Let me go," she asked wearily.

He shook his head and scrutinized her with an intense, unwavering gaze. "You *talk*."

"I . . . no."

"Coward."

Caroline made a plaintive sound of distress. "Without a doubt."

"You gonna leave me just because you're afraid to tell your secrets about animals, yes?"

"Yes."

"You think I'll take advantage of them? Of you?"

"It's not that, no."

He put the tray on a bedside table and came to her quickly. Taking her cold, damp hands, he rubbed his thumbs over her palms and said hoarsely, "Good. I love you, Caroline."

His announcement made her gaze at him in torment. His intense blue eyes refused to give her solace; he demanded answers.

But then he frowned. "Do you love me?" he asked in a low, troubled voice. "I'm talking about the important kind of love. Be honest. No hiding."

Her fingers dug into his. "Blue. I . . . this isn't going to work." He looked so worried that her resolve fell apart and her shoulders slumped. "Yes. *Yes.* I love you."

"*Bien.* That makes the rest easy."

She almost drowned in the rapt pleasure that heated his eyes. Caroline added in a tearful voice, "You're wrong. I'd do anything for you—except live in Louisiana or explain how I work with animals."

He shook his head patiently. "Not good enough. You'll change your mind about staying here. Don't you think I've noticed the moon-eyed way you look at this house and everything around it? You're at home. To hell with the rest of the state."

She gave a strangled laugh. "I grew up wanting desperately to be somebody, and I made it come true. Now I live in a style that most of the world envies. I'm accepted by important people, people with power and money and fame."

She ground her hands against his chest and gazed at him in anguish. "If I live here I'll only be the daughter of an *Américain* fool and a Cajun tramp whose nasty deaths are probably remembered by every old-timer in southern Louisiana."

He grasped her head between his hands and said in a gentle retort, "You'll be Caroline Belue, the lady of Grande Rivage, the lady with a soul so sweet that kids and animals love her at first sight."

Caroline stared at him wordlessly until she found enough breath to speak. "Caroline Belue?"

"I could adopt you, but I think gettin' married would be a better way to change your name." He covered her mouth with one hand. "We'll talk about that later."

She wrenched her head to one side. "No. Didn't you hear anything I just said?"

He sighed. "I don't listen with my ears."

Caroline backed away from him rapidly. He stepped forward and snatched her into his arms. Bending his weathered, rugged face close to hers, he whispered, "It's time we did everything for each other. I want to know how you taste, how you feel under my hands, how those odd, pretty eyes of yours will look when I'm movin' inside you. I want to please you and make you forget everything bad that ever happened to you."

The breath soughed out of her in a soft moan. His voice dropped even lower. "But I can't do that if I don't understand you. Now tell me how you knew that Dulac was using his dog to train pit bulls."

Caroline braced her hands against his chest and ducked her head. "You won't believe me."

He persisted. "Yes, I will. How did you know how Sin got hurt?"

Caroline struggled, shoving at him with both hands. "I'm suffocating. Let me go, let me go. I'll tell you if you let me go."

"Easy, shhh. All right." He released her. She darted

past him and ran to one of the archaic, oversized windows. Caroline snapped the center clasp open and flung both panels wide.

Paul vaulted toward her. "No!"

Caroline gaped at him. "I'm a freak, but I'm n-not a jumping freak!"

He halted, frowning. Breathing roughly and half-crying, she braced her palms on the window facings and drew deep breaths while a night breeze draped the filmy white curtains around her.

Finally he gestured vaguely. "What do you mean, you're a freak?"

"I m-mean . . . oh, hell." Her head sank forward as despair crashed down on her, making it difficult to talk. "I mean that I . . . have a power that nobody will understand or believe." Old bitterness surged into her throat. "You won't either."

"Try me."

"I told my stepparents about it when I was twelve years old. They thought I was lying, that I was trying to get attention. I spent *months* on restriction, and when I kept telling them that I wasn't lying they sent me to a psychiatrist."

"Why, Caro? Caro?"

"Hurts. Wait." She pointed to her throat. Caroline was horrified by the raw, pathetic sorrow in her voice, but she couldn't stop talking. "I don't remember much of the eighth grade because that bastard put me on heavy tranquilizers."

"Oh, *chère*," Paul said hoarsely.

"The worst thing was—" She struggled for composure, covering her face with one hand.

"Caroline," Paul crooned. He moved toward her, his hands outstretched.

"Don't. Stay put. I'll fall apart c-completely if you touch me."

He hesitated, but she could sense how eager he was

to reach for her. *Get it over with,* she told herself. *Then he may not want to hold you.*

"What happened, *chère?*" he asked gently.

Caroline dragged her head up and angled it so he couldn't see the wretched state of her face. "The stupid shrink said I was withdrawing into fantasy because of my scars. He told my stepparents to help me get rid of unhealthy influences.

"I had two pet cats and an old cocker spaniel—my only friends. The shrink said they had to go. I begged my stepparents—I promised to be *perfect* if they'd let the animals stay."

Her voice broke. "My stepparents took them to the humane society. Said they'd get homes." She paused, struggling. "But they didn't. They all got put to sleep."

"Oh, Caro."

"I knew when they were gassed."

"How could you know? Who told you?"

Caroline jammed the heels of her hands against her temples. "It was dark in the gas chamber and they were terrified. The gas was exhaust from an old car engine—not cool or odorless."

"Who told you that?"

"Even miles away I heard them begging me, pleading for help. The fumes burned them, burned their faces. They couldn't breathe, and they were in pain."

Paul groaned in frustration and sorrow. "How did you know?"

Her control shattered. "They told me!" Crumpling, she hugged herself. Tears ran down her face.

There was a sudden stillness in the room, a freezing of both movement and thought. Wincing, Caroline slowly turned to look at Paul.

He gazed back at her as if he'd never seen her before. It was her worst fear come true.

Trembling violently, Caroline drew herself into a weak imitation of her old haughtiness. "'G-give me that damned room key. You won't mind if I leave now.'"

He blinked as if waking up, shoved both hands through his hair, held them up as if beseeching heaven, then let them fall to his sides. "You mean you really do talk to the animals and they talk back?"

"Polite people call it mental telepathy. Impolite people call it a crock."

"I . . . how . . . *mon dieu.*"

"I've always been able to do it. I guess I could even do it before the car accident. I don't know. I can't remember." She wiped her eyes brusquely. "I never told anyone else about it—until now."

Paul waved his hands as if searching for answers and continued to look stunned. "The house cats, the llamas, Wolf, the gazelle, Cat, the ferrets. *Fantastique. Formidable.*"

"Freak," she added grimly.

"What do they say? How do they say it? In words?"

His interest buoyed her a little. "No. Images. Emotions. Except with Wolf. And Sin. With them I speak a language I didn't know I knew. I can't describe it, but it's very detailed."

His eyes flickered with a fathomless emotion. "You 'talk inside their heads,' just like you did with Mark?"

The blood thudded in Caroline's ears. She nodded numbly. "I can communicate only with animals and children."

"Sin *told* you about the pit bulls?"

Caroline looked away awkwardly. "Yes."

He said nothing else, and the silence grew so nerve-racking that she couldn't bear it. Caroline exhaled raggedly. "Okay. I get the message. I thought for a minute . . . no." She swept past him, headed for the door. "Let me out of here. You can laugh after I leave the room."

"You're so damned convinced that I don't believe you." His voice was smooth and challenging. "You're just waiting for me to make fun of you, and you're gonna brood and worry no matter what I say."

He paused. "So there's only one thing to do."

Caroline turned around wearily as he crossed the room to her. "This is no time for accordion music."

He cursed jauntily, snatched her against his torso, sank his hands under her rump, and lifted her on tiptoe so that his hardness slammed into her belly. It was calculated roughness, designed to excite rather than to frighten, and it shattered her overwrought control.

Caroline clutched his shoulders and looked up into his flushed, determined face. His desire and the fervor in his eyes stunned her. Finally she cleared her throat and asked in amazement, "You still want me?"

"I'd still want you if you said that frogs could sing 'Zippity Doo-Dah.'" He shook her lightly. "I love you, Caroline. I believe in you. If you can talk to animals, there's hope for all sorts of good things in the world. There really must be miracles."

Her head swam. "Am I a freak?" she demanded hoarsely.

"Hell, no."

"Do you think I'm crazy, off, bats, one brick short of a load, the elevator doesn't go all the way to the top floor?"

"You've got a gift, Caroline. You're not abnormal, you're *special*. I knew something strange was going on with the animals; I thought that maybe you were psychic, but I kept looking for a better explanation. With all the evidence you gave me, I should have figured out the truth a long time ago."

She felt confused and dazed; suddenly nothing made sense except the admiration in his eyes and the possessive, provocative way he held her against his body. He still wanted to make love to her; he seemed to want it more than ever.

She wound her fingers into his black hair and held tightly. Her eyes unwavering, she asked, "Are you going to tell anyone what I said?"

"No." He looked at her in exasperation, as if these questions were ridiculous but no more than he expected. He bumped her with bawdy skill, his movements an innuendo for much more intimate pastimes. "Is this what it takes to convince you I'm on your side?" he demanded.

Tenderness fought disbelief. Caroline dredged up another stab of cynicism. "Why do you believe me so easily? Are you lying?"

He tilted his head back and groaned dramatically, the sound almost a primitive growl of warning. "No!" Then with a low sound of delight he sank an open-mouthed kiss onto her lips. Caroline arched upward to capture the impatience of it and savor the sweet violence of his tongue. He flicked the tip across her lips, then lifted it to her tear-stained face.

When he licked her cheeks and eyes she fell apart inside and tilted her face for the warm, tender washing. As he ministered to her he carried her to the bed and sat down.

*"Fantastique,"* she murmured as he fell back on the bed and bounced her on his thighs. The giddiness inside her chest broke free as a tentative smile.

Paul growled half in play and half in passion. "There is an animal I want you to talk to."

He lifted his hips into the harbor of her thighs, tantalizing her with the promise of what lay restrained under denim and cotton. His hands drew circles on her lower back, then rose up her spine with tingling slowness and cupped her shoulders.

She shook her head in helpless adoration. "Is it really all right? You believe me?"

He cupped her face reverently. "Oh, Caro, *yes*. Around these old bayous folks grow up believing in mysteries and magic. We Cajuns know better than to doubt things we can't see."

Trembling, she bowed her head. "I never expected acceptance from you."

"You never expected love either."

"No," she agreed softly, and raised her gaze to be mesmerized by his look of devotion. "I'll try my best to show you how much it means to me."

Caroline curled her hands into his sweatshirt, eager to uncover his chest so that she could stroke the black hair and striated muscle. Fumbling as she tried to pull his shirt up, she managed to poke him in the stomach with a lacquered fingernail.

He winced. "Slow, *chère*, slow."

Embarrassed, she stopped. "I'm not much good at this."

"Ooh-la-la, the cat has claws," he teased quickly. "I like them."

"I know how to fake my feelings and I know how to be tender without being sexual," she whispered in dismay, "but I don't know anything in between. Help me."

Quickly the teasing glint faded from his eyes. He pulled the sweatshirt off and threw it across the room, then placed her hands on his chest.

"You're doing fine," he whispered. "'Any better and I'd be a goner.'"

She laughed warily and stroked her fingers down his chest. His hair felt like fine lamb's wool, and the way it hugged the patterns of solid muscle and bones was so hypnotizing that she forgot everything else.

Caroline quivered as she swirled her hands over him, flicking his nipples gently, tracing his collarbones, running her fingers up to his shoulders and down his arms.

He watched her with his eyes half shut, and his chest rose quicker with each passing second. He shifted with pleasure, rotating his hips under her and caressing her sides.

Slowly his hands rose under her breasts, and he cupped them in his palms. His thumbs scrubbed over the tips, making them harden under her dress and bra. She thrust forward instinctively, aching for his touch, and her obvious delight brought a gleam of pure male fire to his eyes.

"This is the way it should be between a man and a woman," he told her. "Gentle and wild at the same time."

"Teach me," she whispered.

Smiling, his face ruddy with desire, he unbuttoned the bodice of her shirtwaist dress and slowly turned the material aside as if he were opening a pretty Christmas present that he wanted to anticipate just a moment longer.

When his forefinger traced a line of sensation from her throat into the cleft of her breasts she was so overcome that she dipped her head and tried to kiss the pleasuring hand. He lifted it to her mouth and she nuzzled his palm.

He groaned. "I don't need to teach you anything, *chère*. You've got so much natural lovin' inside you that you know what to do already. All you need is the chance."

"Please. A chance," she urged.

His heavy-lidded look told her that her words were an aphrodisiac. He slipped his big, nimble fingers into her bodice and lifted it off her shoulders. With quick movements he shoved the soft yellow fabric down to her elbows and ran his fingers over the satiny white bra he'd uncovered.

His hands lingered on her breasts. Gradually he pressed his fingers into the softness and rubbed with a skillful touch that made her pant. Just the idea of feeling his fingers on her bare skin caused her to clutch his sides and shiver.

He smiled wickedly and brushed a finger along the fine lacework edging the cups of her bra. "This is too pretty to be worn. Ought to just hang it up and look at it, eh?"

"Eh," she agreed in a breathless tone. Reaching behind her, her eyes never leaving his, Caroline unfastened the bra. She shrugged gracefully and it slipped down her arms, landing where she placed her hands on his chest.

He held her gaze for a moment, then let his eyes drift down her body. Lusty appreciation deepened his look of barely controlled passion, and she thought if he didn't immediately transfer that look into action, she'd collapse from imagining the results.

He didn't make her wait; he cupped her breasts and raked his thumbs across the taut nipples. When she threw her head back and moaned he sat up and guided her breasts to his mouth.

Caroline laughed with joyous sensation as he gently savaged one nipple and then the other, taunting them to such great sensitivity that each tug of his lips brought a corresponding ache inside her.

She stroked his head fervently, then grasped his shoulders as he bent her backward so that her breasts thrust upward into his mouth.

"I want to do something for you that feels this incredible," she whispered.

He chuckled hoarsely and lay back on the bed, pulling her beside him. Caroline glanced down his magnificent body and smiled at the straining thickness inside his jeans.

"I think I understand," she murmured.

Quickly she unfastened his jeans and slipped her hand inside. Caroline sighed with anticipation. A tremor ran through him and echoed in her own body. His pleasure was hers, and they shared its vibration.

"You're so soft and smooth on the surface, and so hot," she whispered. The light, sensual caress of her fingers made his back bow and his hands tremble.

"Easy, easy," he begged in a barely audible voice. "I haven't got my accordion to protect me."

Her pulse beat a heavy rhythm in her ears. "Your accordion?" she repeated groggily as she uncovered him and watched her hand's caressing motions.

He shut his eyes and swallowed harshly, so lost in sensation that he had trouble responding. Finally he managed to say, "That night. You came up here. Told me . . ." He shifted on the bed. "Aaah, yes, touch me there too." She made a growling sound and he smiled. "You told me to stop playing," he finished.

Caroline nuzzled her face against his stomach. "And you stood in the hall wearing nothing but your squeeze box."

"I wanted you that night, Caroline. I wanted you so bad I woke up aching the next morning."

She cried out happily and kissed the center of his chest. "I wanted you too. I dreamed that I was an accordion and it felt *so* good when you made music with me."

They shared a soft, throaty laugh. His turned into a groan of desire, and he guided her hand up his stomach to more neutral territory. Caroline kissed him and he pulled her close to him.

They both sighed when her nipples brushed against his thickly matted chest. Looking up into her eyes, Paul whispered, "Time to make some music, *chère*."

"The best kind," she answered, her throat tight. "I love you so much."

They undressed each other quickly, all patience gone, and when they finished they stood beside the bed and gazed in rapt silence. "Look, we've got different parts," he murmured coyly, reaching out.

He slid his hand between her legs and cupped her snugly, rubbing his fingers inside the secret folds of her body. Caroline leaned against him, her knees weak. "Have you no shame? Have you no inhibitions?"

"Nah."

She sighed. "Wonderful."

"I'll show you."

He picked her up, laid her on the bed, then eased her knees apart and knelt between them. Caroline lay in expectant silence, her body so infused with languor that she felt too heavy to move.

Without hesitation he ran his hands down her thighs and explored her, making modesty impossible and, more important, unwanted. Caroline writhed, intensely aware of every nerve ending he brought to life. He moved closer, his expression tight with control.

"Got to learn you," he whispered in an urgent tone. "Take it slow. Make a little map."

Readiness surged through her as she felt his hot, velvety tip against her inner thigh. He guided it over the supersensitive skin, tracing her contours in a way that made her legs quiver. Then he performed his special brand of mapmaking on the other thigh.

The harsh rhythm of his breathing excited her beyond anything she could have imagined. She struggled on the bed as he touched himself to the soft center of her body and devoted his attention to that center until only one mystery remained.

Caroline tilted her head back and tried to say how much she loved him, but her control was so far gone that she could only make husky mewling sounds. She felt calm and reckless, loving and lusty in an explosive combination just waiting for the right spark, and she wanted desperately to make this sweet, caring man happy.

"Doc," she finally said, "don't let me embarrass myself. Feeling good is new to me."

"Let's embarrass each other," he urged. "It'll be beautiful."

Paul eased into her body, filling her slowly and completely. Caroline bit her lower lip and fought the desire to writhe. His deep, desire-roughened voice came to her through a haze. "Let go, *chère*. There's no embarrassment here; there's just you and me making love, and everything we do is gonna be our secret to keep."

That was all it took. Caroline made a desperate yearning sound she'd never expected to hear from her own throat. She reached for him with both hands and he lowered himself on top of her, his eyes shining with pleasure at her reaction.

He bent his head and whispered against her ear, "I've found my lifemate, just like Wolf found his, and there won't be another one."

Caroline cried out at the recklessness of these bittersweet promises when so much was unresolved; then she held him tightly and believed every word as her world gave way to Cajun magic.

# Nine

The next few weeks turned her life upside down, and she didn't mind a bit.

She clipped her long fingernails. She tossed most of her jewelry into a drawer of Paul's dresser, where it lay unused, along with her makeup. He drove her to the clothing store in Breaux LaMonde so that she could buy jeans, T-shirts, a floppy straw hat, and utilitarian walking shoes. Her California wardrobe went into Paul's bedroom closet and never came out again.

And she wore sunglasses only when it was sunny.

Word of her romance with Paul spread to all the cast and crew members of *Silver Wolf*; she felt their smiles and curious stares whenever he visited the set, which was every chance he got. The movie's young star, Rebecca, a precocious pint-sized Shirley MacLaine, told her that her aura had turned from black to light blue.

Someone in the crew even swiped her canvas chair with the neatly stenciled *Property of C. Fitzsimmons, Do Not Remove* on its back, and when it reappeared the lettering proclaimed, *Earth Mother and Llama Mama.*

She was delighted.

The world had become a fresh new place full of familiar things that suddenly seemed wondrous—food tasted twice as good, sunsets were twice as beautiful. The air left a sweet scent in her nose and she craved it as if she'd never known how to breathe before.

It was all because of a loving wild man who did things like coax her outside to dance in a lazy afternoon rain, a man who fed her cantaloupe in bed every morning, a man who knew the value of kissing and cuddling and hugging in a warm, deep way that demanded nothing except tenderness.

He brought sick animals to her and watched with silent fascination while she talked them into relaxing; he asked her to act as interpreter between himself and Wolf; he cherished her power and treated it as one more glorious secret they could share.

And she felt not only loved, but beautiful. She couldn't get enough of his company; when they were apart she felt connected to him by an invisible bond of anticipation. When she was with him his lingering touches and frequent glances made it clear that he couldn't get enough of her either.

He used delicious, sometimes bawdy tactics to spark her sensuality, leading by uninhibited example until she cried because she understood what she'd been missing.

Once in the middle of the night she woke moaning from a dream filled with hot, aching sensation. Groggily she realized that Paul was no longer beside her. Then she exclaimed in startled delight as the skilled movements of his tongue told her the dream was real. He was loving her in an incredibly unselfish way.

"Ooh-la-la, look what I found in the dark," he said solemnly.

Simple things became momentous.

"Your café au lait is great," she said at breakfast one morning, and he was so pleased that he made love to her on the kitchen table. As she held him afterward, her face dusted with beignet sugar and her fingers languidly rubbing the remnants of grape jelly into his naked rump, she sensed the presence of the house cats.

Paul had his face burrowed in the crook of her neck, where he was licking up a trace of strawberry preserves. She nuzzled his hair gratefully, then looked over at the feline visitors. They sat on the windowsill, watching with dignified disapproval.

She burst into giggles. Paul lifted his head and smiled at her. He had a dollop of honey on one eyebrow. Caroline laughed harder, and he arched into her jiggling body.

"Whatever's so funny, keep thinking about it," he said rakishly.

"The c-cats," she sputtered. "They think we're silly."

He glanced quickly toward the window. "Hey, purrs." Then he looked back at Caroline. "Why?"

"Because we're playing in our food."

Rich laughter rolled from his throat. "Tell them I like to play in my food before I eat it." And as she stared at him with a stunned, giddy grin, he slid down her body and began licking sugar from her navel, Caroline let her head fall back onto a crushed beignet and sighed with delight.

*Silver Wolf* finished filming in two weeks. Two weeks were two centuries when every second vibrated with life, and the future was no more than a vague shadow in a distant mist.

Wearing only her black Oriental robe, Caroline strolled off the back veranda and stood in the gray-tinted darkness just before dawn, gazing contentedly at the morning star. Paul's grueling days always started at this time, and her night-owl heart had finally adjusted.

She smiled wryly. Only the deepest kind of love could make her enjoy getting up at these hours to be with him.

"What you doin', *chère*? Calling the birds for breakfast?"

He came out the back door and strolled barefoot off the veranda to her, running a hand over his chest, then stretching like some magnificent panther just waking up.

Caroline put her arms around his bare waist and smiled up at him. "I thought you were taking a shower." She tugged lightly at the waist of his white pajama bottoms. "You weren't wearing these last time I saw you."

"I was supposed to have company in the shower, yes?"

"I heard a strange noise out here. Like a deep grunt."

He gave her an exasperated look. "So you just brought your fearless fanny downstairs alone to investigate."

"No animal would hurt me."

He glanced around, frowning. "Where's Wolf and Sin?"

"Asleep on their blankets in the parlor. Oh, I meant to tell you. Her name's *Lady* now, not Sin. She agreed that it was more appropriate."

He arched a black brow rakishly. "Givin' the animals fancy names, eh? Next she'll want a rhinestone collar."

Caroline chuckled. "You're *not* going to name her She-Dog. I protest."

A deep bellow punctured the night so close by that Caroline jumped and looked around her feet. Paul swung about, gazing at the veranda intensely.

" 'Gator," he said in a troubled voice. "That's the grunt you heard. Must be Big Daddy. He's the only 'gator tame enough to come this close to people."

Caroline's gaze followed his to a large hole torn in the white wooden slats at the veranda's base. She shut her eyes and concentrated. "Uhm-huh. He's under the veranda. He, uhmm, aha!"

She patted Paul's back sympathetically. "Doc, Big Daddy is Big Mama."

"*Mais non!*" He stared at her as if she'd just accused John Wayne of being a sissy.

"*Mais oui.* She's avoiding an overaggressive boyfriend."

He ran a hand through his hair and massaged the scar on the back of his neck. Caroline watched the odd, troubled gesture and was puzzled. "She'll leave when it gets light, doc. What's the matter?"

"Get her out *now.*"

Startled, she told him, "She won't go. She's not in the mood."

He cursed darkly and headed back inside the house, slapping one hand along his thigh in disgust. Caroline followed anxiously.

In the kitchen he paced back and forth, and once again he raised a hand to rub the back of his neck. She settled slowly in a chair and watched him.

"I never told you how I got hurt," he said.

Caroline nodded vaguely, bewildered by the sudden change of subject. She knew his scar by heart, just as he knew hers. It was an upturned crescent at the base of his skull, a dramatic ridge almost the width of her hand.

"An alligator did it?"

"No, no 'gator."

"You haven't seemed eager to tell me," she explained. "So I didn't pry. I knew you'd tell me eventually. What happened?"

He exhaled wearily. "When I was working at the track in New Orleans I got kicked by a horse."

"In the back of the head?"

"Yeah. Nearly killed me." He paused in his restless movements and looked at her with eyes full of old memories. "Bruised my spinal cord. I was paralyzed for about two months. From the neck down."

Caroline hunched over in her chair and hugged her

suddenly queasy stomach. "Oh, doc. No wonder you don't like to talk about it." Tears came to her eyes. "And all the times you've listened patiently to me complain about my scar—"

"Shhh. The hell I went through didn't last for years like yours did."

"But you were *paralyzed*."

"Yeah. It was . . . I wouldn't wish it on anyone. It's what got me thinking about my life. It made me change directions. When I got well I bought this place."

They heard Big Mama bellow again. Paul's expression went darker than before. "Dammit, see if you can get her out from under the house."

"I can't. She's not hurting anything. What's wrong?"

His jaw worked for a moment. He looked at her awkwardly, then announced, "It's bad luck for a 'gator to crawl under your house."

"Ah."

"That was a what-a-cute-Cajun-superstition ah. Dammit, take me seriously."

Caroline spread her hands in a gesture of reconciliation. "Now, doc—"

"I got kicked in the head a week after a 'gator crawled under my house in N'Orleans."

She gaped at him for a minute. So *that* was the cause of his sudden mood change. "Doc, it's just coincidence."

He glared at her. "I never questioned what you told me about talkin' to animals, but you think what I'm saying about superstition is silly, yes?"

Caroline blushed. "I think you're overreacting."

"Then you don't understand Cajuns."

A cold thread of resistance wound through her. "I never said that I did."

"Or that you wanted to."

Caroline stood, alarmed. There was only one possible explanation for his sudden anger. "You're upset about the film shoot coming to an end so soon now."

He held her eyes, searching them. Then he said gruffly, "Frank told me last night that you'll have to take Wolf to film some scenes at the studio in Burbank. You knew that a week ago. Why didn't you tell me?"

Caroline slumped back into the chair and looked at him wretchedly. "I didn't want to spoil the mood."

His anger dimmed a little. Sighing, he slowly nodded, admitting that she had been wise. Then his gaze hardened again. "That 'gator, he . . . *she's* a bad sign. I don't want you to go."

Her throat taut with unshed tears, Caroline whispered, "Doc, I have to go. But I'll be back."

"To stay for good?"

She shook her head. "To visit." She looked at him with anguish. "I love you and I don't want to lose you. We'll work something out even if I live in California and you live here."

"This is your home!"

Crying silently now, she shook her head. "No."

"I thought you'd changed."

"I have. I love you and I love this place. If I could transplant it and you to California, I'd be the happiest woman in the world."

"Transplant yourself *here.*"

"I refuse to live in the same state with my mother's family. Dammit, it's beneath me. It's a point of principle. I thought you'd accepted that."

"Pride!" he yelled. "Stupid pride! I don't understand how you can love me so much and want to live all the way across the damned country."

"I don't want to live across the country, but I can't get you to leave Louisiana!" She held out her hands to him. "Paul, it'll work. It's not traditional, but it *will* work. I'll visit, I'll call, I'll write."

"I don't want a pen pal, I want a wife."

She shook her fists at him. "You want everything your own way!"

They stared at each other, lost in a gulf filled with shared pride and sorrow. Big Mama bellowed again.

Paul waved a hand toward the veranda. "Go hide with her."

Caroline groaned with frustration. "You don't give up."

"I do when I'm beating my head against a stone levee." He pivoted abruptly and left the room.

The old man drove an ancient, rusting pickup truck onto the set and staggered out of it before the crew's security guard noticed him. He tripped over a tree root and fell to one knee, then splayed his arms out and pushed his tall, skinny frame up like a scarecrow.

"Caroline!" he yelled in a heavy Cajun accent.

Everything ground to a halt. "Cut!" the director yelled in disgust. Frederick, Dabney, and Wolf looked at the man curiously.

Caroline, sitting in her chair just outside the bustle of activity, stared at the old man in astonishment. Lady rose from her place under the chair and took a watchful position. Wolf trotted over and stood beside her.

*Mistress, don't be afraid. He doesn't have badness in his face.*

The old man swayed and swept bleary eyes around the set. Wearing faded overalls and a baggy print shirt, his graying red hair sticking out at odd angles, he looked like a skinny Red Skelton playing Clem Cadiddlehopper.

"Where's *ma petite-fille*?" he shouted, looking distressed.

*Granddaughter.* Caroline dropped the script and clutched the arms of her chair. Horror sleeted through her and made her mouth taste brassy with fear. Oh, dear Lord, no.

She stood up, her knees weak, and stared at the invader in numb despair. The security guard grabbed him by one arm.

"Lemme go, you crazy coot," the old man protested, "I got to see my grandbaby! I heard she's here, yes! You *Américain's* can't hide her no more!" He waved his arms and slurred a litany of colorful oaths, half in English and half in Cajun French.

Suddenly Frank was beside Caroline, a supporting hand under her elbow. "He's drunk, Carrie."

"Get him *out* of here," she whispered, her throat a dry well of humiliation. "How did he find me? Why did he find me? Oh, God, he's my worst nightmare."

"Where is she? I'd know her. She had her mama's hair and eyes! Caroline! I'm your kin!" He took a loose swing at the guard and missed.

Caroline pressed her hands to her mouth. She felt the crew's furtive, embarrassed glances and wanted to sink into the ground. She needed her sunglasses again, desperately. She was a violent old drunkard's granddaughter, and she wanted to hide in shame.

"Let's take him to my trailer," Frank said gently. "We'll give him some coffee and—"

"*No,*" she said harshly.

"Carrie—"

"Get him off this place." She tilted a little. "Frank, I feel sick."

The security guard wrestled with the old man, whose rolled-up shirt-sleeves revealed strong, corded forearms. The guard's face turned red with exertion. A cameraman ran over and grabbed her grandfather's free arm.

The guard called, "What do you want me to do with him, Mr. Windham?"

"*Petite-fille!*" her grandfather called plaintively. He glanced around wildly, his gaze stopping on Caroline. "You're her! Oh, Lord, those eyes. Michelle! My baby!"

Caroline staggered back, jerked her arm away from

Frank's grasp, and turned blindly. "I'll be at the house." she said between gasping breaths.

"Carrie."

She groaned. "I can't take it."

Caroline strode away, Wolf and Lady at her heels.

"Don't go!" the old man yelled. "Michelle, don't go! It's Papa!"

She walked faster, her hands knotted, her head down.

His voice rose into a begging cry. "It's Papa . . . *non, merci*, grandpapa! I come to see you! You're my blood!"

Humiliation overwhelmed her and she ran.


Paul slid to a stop in the grand old foyer and looked around frantically. The sound of canine feet rushing across the hardwood floor above him drew his searching eyes to the staircase. Wolf and Lady careened to a stop at the edge of the landing and whined at him anxiously.

"Caroline!"

His heart thudding, he raced up the stairs and entered his bedroom. She was sitting in a big claw-footed chair that faced the window. Paul knelt beside it and studied her sympathetically. Her shoulders were hunched with tension and she'd slipped tortoiseshell-framed sunglasses over her eyes.

Tears escaped from under them as she looked at him. "Where is he? Did he leave?"

Paul cupped a hand around the back of her head and stroked her golden-red hair as if she were a distraught child. "His name's Jacque. Jacque Ancelet. Frank sent the guard to drive him home. He lives over in Juliette. 'Bout an hour west of here. He read a newspaper story on the movie and saw your name. That's all I could get from him before he passed out."

She turned to look out the window again, silent tears sliding down her face. "I have to go see him."

Paul felt a stab of dread. "*Chère*, no."

"You've always said I need to know the truth about my mother's family."

He squeezed the back of her neck, massaging, coaxing. "Not this truth. This'll only be bad."

She wiped trembling fingertips across her cheeks. Even behind her sunglasses he could see her frown of bewilderment. "You told me not to trust rumors."

"Jacque is no rumor. He's flesh and blood." Paul turned her face to him and clasped it between his hands. "He's no good. So what? You've got a home here. I love you. The animals love you. Forget about your mother's family."

She shook her head gently. "I have to go see them, Blue."

Paul got up and paced, his hands on his hips. "No. It's gonna be bad. You'll go back to California for sure."

"Why are you so upset?"

He halted, his hands clenching. "The alligator. She's a bad sign. I told you."

"Oh, Paul!"

"It's not just superstition," he said between gritted teeth. "It means something. It means don't go see your mother's people."

She stood wearily, gripping the back of the chair for support. "Unless I find out what kind of family I came from, I don't know if I can ever stay here."

His head drooped in defeat. "What if they're even worse than you thought?"

"I don't know what I'll do." She came to him and stroked his face tenderly, her hands quivering. "But I know it won't change how much I love you."

Paul drew a deep breath and said grimly, "Right now I feel like locking the door again and holding you prisoner until you say you won't do this foolish thing. You'll always be my woman, and that's all that matters."

He stepped back. She looked up at him mutely, sorrow written in every line of her body. "It'll be all right, doc."

"I'll take you to see them," he whispered, his voice gruff. "Even if it means I lose you."

Caroline's hands went ice cold when she saw the dusty streets and quaint old storefronts of Juliette. She gripped the armrest on the Corvette's passenger door, then used the other hand to check her white-rimmed sunglasses and matching scarf. Slipping a finger under the high, banded neck of her dress, she tugged it upward.

"You're well hidden, *chère*," Paul said drolly, the wind whipping his words. "And you look rich and important. Relax."

Caroline smoothed the draped jersey of her dress, chic and charcoal-gray, meant to impress without shouting for attention. She lifted a heavy necklace of silver crescents and looked at Paul anxiously. "Simple but elegant."

He gestured at his black trousers and white pullover. "Simple but plain."

Caroline chuckled despite her nervousness. "There's nothing plain about you, *monsieur*."

Her laughter died as he turned off the highway and guided the Corvette down a two-lane road bordered on both sides by flat expanses of marsh. In the distance she saw a grove of cypress trees and a small frame house among them.

A chill ran down her spine. "That must be it."

Paul glanced at the directions he'd gotten from the security guard who'd driven Jacque Ancelet home. He slowed the Corvette. "There are lots of cars in the yard. He must have company. Maybe we should have called. Maybe we should go back to town and call. Or go back to Grande Rivage and come again some other day."

"No, Blue. I knew there were going to be lots of people here."

Paul swung the Corvette onto the side of the road and stopped a few hundred feet from the graveled driveway. "How did you know?"

"I called my grandfather and told him that I was coming to see him today. I asked him to invite any of the family who wanted to meet me."

Paul groaned. "What did he say?"

"He's sort of shy, I think. He just mumbled something and said he'd do it." She sat in silent melancholy for a moment, then said with a trace of her old sarcasm, "A house full of crummy Ancelets. Lovely. I'll get the whole rotten picture in one day and then I won't have to see any of them again."

"You don't have to see any of them *now*."

Tears sprang to her eyes and she lifted his hand to kiss it. "Shhh. No matter how awful they are, I'll always want to be a part of *your* life. I love you too much for anything else to matter."

He smiled sadly. "You love me but you'll go back to California."

She shut her eyes and took a deep breath. "Let's get it over with."

The house was basic clapboard and tin, but surprisingly well kept. The mild Louisiana fall let red geraniums continue to bloom in whitewashed truck tires. The ersatz planters were sunk in a sandy yard that bore broom marks where someone had tidied the ground. Caroline studied a porch hung with pots of begonias and furnished with metal lawn chairs painted blue.

Her knees trembled as she crossed the yard. Paul's hand was a strong, calm support on the small of her back. She swallowed tightly as a screen door swung open and Jacque Ancelet stepped onto the porch, his eyes already riveted to her.

Caroline felt Paul's hand curl around her waist protectively. He drew her close to his side and whispered, "Anytime you want to leave, just say so."

She nodded. Her stomach twisted with a confusing mixture of distaste and pity. Jacque looked terribly awkward in an old blue suit that fit too loosely over the angles of his tall, skinny form. His feathery red hair was slicked back, and his face had the pink scrubbed look of a man who equated cleanliness with important occasions.

The more important, the harder he scrubbed, she suspected. Why was he trying so hard to impress the granddaughter he'd forgotten years before?

Caroline's mouth flattened in a grim line as people bustled onto the porch behind him, all gazing at her with mingled curiosity and concern. She'd never seen so many shades of reddish-blond hair in her life. Here and there she noticed features that reminded her of her own—sassily tilted mouths, big dramatic eyes that dominated the rest of the face, chins just a little on the belligerent side.

The crowd was as wholesome-looking as a church choir, and the collection of cars and trucks they'd left among the cypress trees were sparkling late models or older ones in respectable condition.

Confusion brought a surge of anger. Just because they weren't ne'er-do-wells didn't mean they were likable.

Her grandfather walked down the steps and stopped in front of her, his Adam's apple bobbing with nervousness. He was a big scarecrow of a man, but there was a sense of dignity about the squared set of his shoulders.

"I hope a crazy old *grand-père* didn't embarrass you too much," he said in heavily accented English.

Caroline asked grimly, "Are you an alcoholic?"

"No. I'm a coward."

"Uncle, shhh, that's not true," a man in the crowd said.

Jacque shook his head in disagreement, his gaze never leaving Caroline. "I was scared to see my granddaughter again. 'Fraid she'd turned into an *Américaine*. So I had a few drinks." He paused, frowning deeply. "I forgot that it don't set too well with me."

"He hadn't had a drink in ten years," someone said.

Caroline knotted her hands together tensely. "I don't understand why you bothered to come see me when you hadn't tried since I was a child."

"Those damned Fitzsimmonses told you a bunch of lies!" Jacque said, his face flushed with anger.

"Of course you'd say that."

"They took you off to Connecticut and wouldn't let us see you! I went up there!" Jacque waved a hand toward the crowd behind him. "François, Annie, Sebastien—they went too. But your daddy's people had a judge in their pocket and he said us backwoods Cajuns weren't good enough for you, no!"

A stout older woman came forward and shook Jacque's arm. She looked at Caroline somberly. "The judge, he says your daddy's people can give you a better life. He says seeing us would only upset you, 'cause you had brain damage."

Caroline gasped, "I never had brain damage! And your story doesn't make sense, because my father's people didn't want me! Why would they fight you for custody?"

Jacque shook his fists in the air, the gesture so much like her own fist-shaking tendencies that Caroline was stunned.

"They just didn't want a bunch of Cajuns to raise a Fitzsimmons!"

"Can you blame them after what my mother did?"

Jacque's mouth worked vigorously before he mastered enough control to get words out. "Your *maman*'s only crime was loving an *Américain* who had more pride than sense!"

The woman beside Jacque frowned in reproach. "Johnny was a good boy. Don't you tell his daughter nonsense." She looked at Caroline. "I'm your cousin Riva."

"He had to have everything perfect!" Jacque insisted. "He had to have money! He didn't know what was important!"

"He wanted Michelle to have the best, *Grand-père*," Riva corrected him.

Caroline hushed them with impatiently raised hands. "She had an affair. She deserted him. I heard that story all my life."

"Doesn't mean it's true," Paul interjected hopefully.

Caroline trembled with the need to restore order to her beliefs. "Then why would my father's people hate her so much?"

" 'Cause she spoke her mind and she knew what was best for her husband," Riva replied.

"She chased other men," Caroline said hoarsely.

"She liked to talk and she never met a stranger, man or woman," Jacque admitted. "But any man said she was flirtin' with him, he was just doin' some wishful thinking." His eyes flared. "Her only fault was that she was faithful to her crazy husband!"

The crowd of Ancelet relatives had been growing agitated as they listened to the debate. It was obvious that they had words to contribute to the discussion and they couldn't be politely silent any longer. They swirled off the porch to surround Caroline and Paul.

"I'm your uncle François. Your mama and daddy loved each other. You believe it."

"I'm Clarisse, your great-aunt. We always wondered how you were. We thought you had it good, that you probably didn't want anything to do with us."

Another chimed in, "Why didn't you come see us before now?"

Caroline faltered, feeling trapped by their fervent attention. "I don't know." She shook her head, clearing it. "I mean, I was taught to hate my mother and her people. Why would I want to see you?"

"Don't think we desert our own! We wanted you!"

"We heard that you could get better surgeons for your face in Connecticut."

"We heard your daddy's people gave you everything a little girl dreams about."

"Oh, God," Caroline said weakly.

Paul tightened his arm around her and eyed the crowd with reproach. "Go easy. You can't change her feelings by overwhelming her."

Caroline jerked her sunglasses off and flung them on the ground. She pointed to her scar and watched everyone's stunned reaction. "Why do I have this? If my parents were so damned wonderful, how did this happen?"

"Oh, *petite*," Jacque said hoarsely. "My poor *petite-fille*,"

"I don't want your sympathy, I want explanations! Did my mother get drunk and drive head-on into a tractor-trailer, or not? Explain that!"

"Your *maman* had just one beer!"

"The road was slick. It was raining."

"It was an accident. She was upset; she was driving too fast."

Caroline gritted her teeth in frustration. "Why was she upset?"

"Your daddy wanted her to leave him!"

"Whoa, whoa." Caroline swayed, feeling like a dazed boxer trying to dodge a knockout punch. "He wanted *what*?"

Her grandfather grasped her hands. Without thinking, she clung to his gentle, calloused fingers. His eyes were full of tears.

"That boy said he was no good for her because he lost all his money in some sort of get-rich-quick deal.

Had to sell their big house, jewelry he'd given her, everything, and take a cheap apartment. He drove her away because he didn't want her to see him poor. She came back here with you, but she begged him to come too. Finally he came out to see her and you. They—" He stopped, swallowing hard.

"They cried and they argued," Riva continued. "I was here. Your *grand-mère* Ancelet was alive then, too, and we both heard. Your *maman* says you and her are going back to N'Orleans with him. He says no—he had so much pride, your daddy—he says she can't come back until he can give you two all the nice things you had before."

Jacque cleared his throat roughly. "She says she's going to the apartment where she belongs and he can't stop her. So she got in the car with you and left. Your daddy went after her."

Caroline felt her grandfather's grip tighten. She realized abruptly that Paul had both arms around her and that she was crying. "And he found us in the accident."

"*Oui.*"

"And later, he . . . felt so guilty . . ."

"He loved you both so much," Riva said in a trembling voice. "He just couldn't take what he'd done to you."

Caroline shook her head. "I can't believe any of this. It's too much, too soon. You can't expect—"

"There's plenty of time, Caro," Paul murmured, kissing her temple. He sounded enormously relieved. His lips brushed over her scar. "It takes time to heal." After a second he added, "And to forget about alligators."

Jacque tugged on her hands. "Come inside. See my scrapbooks. I've got pictures of your *maman*." He paused, then added reluctantly, "And your papa."

She was so unnerved by all the claims she'd just heard about her parents, she knew nothing she said would make sense. "What do you want me to do?"

Paul shook her gently. "Just go inside and sit down, *chère.*"

"You don't know us very well yet," Riva told her. "And we don't know you. But we *want* you to be part of the family. It's a good family. You'll see."

Caroline looked up woozily at the man who still held her so protectively. "I have you."

He nodded, his eyes reassuring her with their strength and calmness. "And now you've got a whole bunch of other Cajuns, too, eh? Let's go see some scrapbooks."

Caroline sat stiffly on an old divan with Paul next to her. She kept turning her flushed face toward the cooling breeze from an open window nearby. She felt like the center of attention at a celebrity roast.

Only she was the stand-in for the real guests of honor, her mother and father, and the speeches were being given by relatives who told loving anecdotes, not jokes.

But it did no good. She felt hollow, a breathing, nodding, listening mannequin whose only clear thought was that the scene and the words couldn't be real. The stories she heard didn't register because the shock was still too great.

Her parents were distant, blurred figures who'd lost their well-defined shape in her imagination. She kept trying to rearrange them into believable new images— her father brash, proud, and ambitious but also incredibly decent and loving, her mother impetuous and naive but favored with a special sort of warmth that compelled devotion from everyone who knew her.

It couldn't be done. They were lost to her by too many years of anger and pain.

Caroline looked wearily at an uncle or cousin or something—she couldn't keep track anymore—who was talking about her father's attempts to learn Cajun French just to please his new wife. She concentrated as hard as she could, but his words had no effect on her shell-shocked emotions.

Jacque, who sat majestically in the middle of the crowd, his lanky body folded into a creaky chair, suddenly pounded the armrest. "What you doin'?" he shouted, frowning. "Get away from that window!"

Caroline glanced distractedly over her shoulder. All her senses snapped back to life.

*Apples?* the old mule asked, his grizzled gray lips flapping comically as he tried to nibble her sleeve. *Apples? I missed you. Where have you been?*

"Get out of that window, Otis!" Jacque got up and strode over, flapping his arms. Otis snorted and withdrew quickly.

Caroline held her breath and twisted on the divan to peer after the mule. *Otis? How do you know me?*

He stood outside, looking up at her with huge, hopeful dark eyes. *Apples,* he repeated firmly. *When I was small. You know when I hurt. You know when I sad. You give apples.*

Caroline dimly realized that her grandfather was wiping mule saliva off the sleeve of her dress.

"I'm sorry," he said gruffly. "He hasn't done that in years. Your *maman* taught him to stick his head in the window."

Caroline latched onto the divan's armrest with one shaking hand and turned to look at Paul. He straightened anxiously when he saw the expression on her face.

"Caro? What's wrong?"

Her eyes never leaving Paul's, she asked her grandfather. "Did my mother feed Otis apples?"

Jacque chuckled, obviously relieved by her lack of annoyance. "All the time. I got him the year before she married your papa. He was just six months old, and she treated him like a baby." His hands halted on her sleeve. "How did you know about the apples?"

Understanding came into Paul's gaze. His lips parted in a stunned smile. "Tell them, Caro."

She turned slowly to look into Jacque's bewildered expression. "Did my mother have a . . . a way with animals?"

His mouth dropped open. Caroline heard gasps from others in the room. Suddenly Jacque grabbed her arms. "You've got it too! You've got *la touche chaude*. The hot touch. She could touch an animal or even just look at it and tell you what it was thinking!"

Caroline looked at her relatives' excited faces. "You all believe that? Really? You didn't think she was making it up?"

"I saw her tell 'gators which way to crawl, and they'd do it!" one said.

"Wild birds would land on her hands!" another added.

Riva stood up proudly. "When Michelle went to Connecticut to meet your papa's family, she got in a terrible fight with somebody who was mean to a cat. I'll never forget how upset she was when she told me about it. She said the cat told her awful things about being pinched and stuff."

Caroline clutched Paul's hand. "That was Grandmother Fitzsimmons' cat." She looked at her grandfather again. "What did you call it? Her talent?"

"*La touche chaude*," he repeated hoarsely, smiling. "The hot touch."

Breathing raggedly, she turned toward Paul. He leaned forward and kissed her. The love in his eyes released tears that slid down her face and over her bittersweet smile. "I'm not alone," she whispered brokenly.

There were tears in his eyes too. Around them people were crying openly. Her grandfather put one big, angular hand on her head and stroked awkwardly.

"You never have been, *petite*," he murmured. "You just didn't know it."

The canopy of oaks at Grande Rivage arched over

them like adoring friends. Caroline cradled Paul's hand in hers as they walked up the road. The old mansion sat at the end, looking more beautiful than a run-down place in need of her loving attention had a right to look.

Caroline laughed softly. "Wonderful."

"Talking to some animal I don't see?" Paul teased. He put his arm around her and drew her to him.

Caroline looked up into his face and didn't speak for a moment, enjoying the rush of pleasure she felt when she lost herself in his eyes.

"Thank you for indulging my need to walk," she whispered. They'd left the Corvette near the end of the driveway.

Paul caressed her face tenderly. "It's been a long, strange day. The walk feels good." He cupped her chin in one hand and studied her face. "How are you, *chère*? The truth."

"Better," she said in a thoughtful tone. "Much better than I've ever been in my life. And peaceful."

*"Bien."* Stepping back, he took her hands in his and looked at her with a quiet intensity that sent tingles up her spine. "Mademoiselle Caroline, will you marry a Cajun veterinarian who doesn't care about being rich or living fancy but who'll love you like no other man on the face of the earth?"

Caroline squinted at the trees overhead as if thinking. "I believe I'm as smart as my mother," she said finally. "I know what's important." She looked at Paul so raptly that he began to smile.

"Say it," he whispered.

She brought his hands to her lips. "I'll marry you," she answered, kissing them. "You're my lifemate and I'll never want anyone else."

They stood in the driveway a long time, just holding each other. Long golden shadows slanted through the oaks when she and Paul finally walked into the yard, savoring every moment of a glorious fall sunset.

Wolf and Lady rose from a cushion on the veranda. They crossed the lawn, tails wagging, and Lady pranced a little. Caroline gasped softly and began to laugh.

"What?" Paul asked.

She stopped and took his hands. "We're going to be godparents."

"*Bien!*" He looked at Wolf and Lady with an approving smile. "You're trying to set a good example for us to follow, yes?"

Caroline smiled through tears of joy. "It's their way of giving us an engagement present."

Paul put his arm around her, and together they watched Wolf come forward alone. He stopped in front of them and gazed from Paul to her, his dark silver eyes gleaming with a contentment that spoke to the center of her heart.

*No more sadness. Welcome home.*

# THE EDITOR'S CORNER

This month we're inaugurating a special and permanent feature that is dear to our hearts. From now on we'll spotlight one Fan of the Month at the end of the Editor's Corner. Through the years we've enjoyed and profited from your praise, your criticisms, your analyses. So have our authors. We want to share the joy of getting to know a devoted romance reader with all of you other devoted romance readers—thus, this feature. We hope you'll enjoy getting to know our first Fan of the Month, Pat Diehl.

Our space is limited this month due to the addition of our new feature, so we can give you only a few tasty tidbits about each upcoming book.

Leading off is Kay Hooper with LOVESWEPT #360, **THE GLASS SHOE,** the second in her *Once Upon a Time* series. This modern Cinderella story tells the tale of beautiful heiress Amanda Wilderman and dashing entrepreneur Ryder Foxx, who meet at a masquerade ball. Their magical romance will enchant you, and the fantasy never ends—not even when the clock strikes midnight!

Gail Douglas is back with *The Dreamweavers*: **GAMBLING LADY,** LOVESWEPT #361, also the second in a series. Captaining her Mississippi riverboat keeps Stefanie Sinclair busy, but memories of her whirlwind marriage to Cajun rogue T.J. Carriere haunt her. T.J. never understood what drove them apart after only six months, but he vows to win his wife back. Stefanie doesn't stand a chance of resisting T.J.—and neither will you!

LOVESWEPT #362, **BACK TO THE BEDROOM** by Janet Evanovich, will have you in stitches! For months David Dodd wanted to meet the mysterious woman who was always draped in a black cloak and carrying a large, odd case—and he finally gets the chance when a helicopter drops a chunk of metal through his lovely neighbor's roof and he rushes to her rescue. Katherine Finn falls head over heels for David, but as a dedicated concert musician, she can't fathom the man who seems to be drifting through life. This wonderful story is sure to strike a chord with you!

Author Fran Baker returns with another memorable romance, **KING OF THE MOUNTAIN,** LOVESWEPT #363. Fran deals with a serious subject in **KING OF THE MOUNTAIN,** and she handles it beautifully. Heroine Kitty
*(continued)*

Reardon carries deep emotional scars from a marriage to a man who abused her, and hero Ben Cooper wants to offer her sanctuary in his arms. But Kitty is afraid to reach out to him, to let him heal her soul. This tenderly written love story is one you won't soon forget.

Iris Johansen needs no introduction, and the title of her next LOVESWEPT, #364, **WICKED JAKE DARCY,** speaks for itself. But we're going to tantalize you anyway! Mary Harland thinks she's too innocent to enchant the notorious rake Jake Darcy, but she's literally swept off her feet by the man who is temptation in the flesh. Dangerous forces are at work, however, forcing Mary to betray Jake and begin a desperate quest. We bet your hearts are already beating in double-time in anticipation of this exciting story. Don't miss it!

From all your cards and letters, we know you all just love a bad-boy hero, and has Charlotte Hughes got one for you in **SCOUNDREL,** LOVESWEPT #365. Growing up in Peculiar, Mississippi, Blue Mitchum had been every mother's nightmare, and every daughter's fantasy. When Cassie Kennard returns to town as Cassandra D'Clair, former world-famous model, she never expects to encounter Blue Mitchum again—and certainly never guessed he'd be mayor of the town! Divorced, the mother of twin girls, Cassie wants to start a new life where she feels safe and at home, but Blue's kisses send her into a tailspin! These two people create enough heat to singe the pages. Maybe we should publish this book with a warning on its cover!

Enjoy next month's LOVESWEPTs and don't forget to keep in touch!

Sincerely,

*Carolyn Nichols*

Carolyn Nichols
Editor
*LOVESWEPT*
Bantam Books
666 Fifth Avenue
New York, NY 10103

**LOVESWEPT IS PROUD
TO INTRODUCE OUR FIRST
FAN OF THE MONTH**

**Pat Diehl**

I was speechless when Carolyn Nichols called to say she wanted me to be LOVESWEPT's first **FAN OF THE MONTH,** but I was also flattered and excited. I've read just about every LOVESWEPT ever published and have corresponded with Carolyn for many years. I own over 5,000 books, which fill two rooms in my house. LOVESWEPT books are "keepers," and I try to buy them all and even get them autographed. Sometimes I reread my favorites—I've read **LIGHTNING THAT LINGERS** by Sharon and Tom Curtis twenty-seven times! Some of my other favorite authors are Sandra Brown, Joan Elliott Pickart, Billie Green, and Mary Kay McComas, but I also enjoy reading the new authors' books.

Whenever I come across a book that particularly moves me, I buy a copy, wrap it in pretty gift paper, and give it to a senior citizen in my local hospital. I intend to will all my romance books to my granddaughter, who's now two years old. She likes to sit next to me and hold the books in her hands as if she were reading them. It's possible that there could be another **FAN OF THE MONTH** in the Diehl family in the future!